THE ISLE OF LIES

THE ISLE OF LIES

M.P. SHIEL

Originally published in 1908.

Published by Wildside Press, LLC.
Visit us online at wildsidepress.com.

CHAPTER I.

THE STELE.

Perhaps one's happiest manner to begin the history of the remarkable boy whose moral we have to point is to give, as we can, that part of Professor S. S. Reid's diary which has to do with the matter. The professor writes:

* * * *

I have this morning the tidings that a son is born to Dr. Lepsius, and as the fact may possibly come to prove momentous in the history of experiment, I am about now to jot down just what I was in the way to know of the story.

In the dog-days of '68, close on two years gone now, our bout-at-arms with Theodore III. of Abyssinia came to a close with the capture of Magdala by Napier: and the victory was still in everyone's mouth, when Lepsius one afternoon strolls into my study to notify me that the British Government was about to send out a mission to that country, and that he, Lepsius, was to accompany it in some rôle or other. I was quite surprised, in spite of my familiarity with the manifold activities of this man.

"*You* going to Abyssinia?" I exclaimed.

"I am," says he.

"But what for?" I asked.

"There are the Jurassic limestones for one thing," he answered, "and you surely know that some more or less valuable MSS., especially Bible MSS., already derive from Abyssinia."

He then proceeded to tell me that in the rage of the Mohammedan invasion of that region in the sixteenth century, the Abyssinians heaped most of their Ethiopian and other manuscripts into a certain museum on Debra-Seena (an island of Lake Sana), where they remain guarded by clerics, who regard them as idol relics. "Abyssinia, then," said he, "might not be a bad four-months' abode for a bloke like me; at all events, I am off."

What surprises me is that a man like Lepsius, a tender wight at bottom surely, should have let himself become the excuse for bloodshed during this exuberance of his, and should have been led into committing an act which the common man might well consider wonderfully like pilfer-

1

ing—at the spur of a whim! Learning, may be, has a claim to make its own code of morals, but I am convinced that in, say, Madrid, Lepsius would have shrunk with dismay from doing what in that savage country he did with the coolest self-assurance.

The mission reached the town of Gondar at the end of August—a world of mountains now, after a camel-journey of some weeks across the lowlands from Somaliland. By September, Dr. Lepsius had won sufficient favour for his purposes with the viceroy, or *ras*, and, with his usual rashness, ventured out with only one Choan servant on an ass for Lake Sana, twenty miles south, to examine the MSS., etc.

It appears that in these regions the rainy season is from June to the tail-end of September, so that now it was pouring without pity. However, one forenoon Lepsius comes to the lake, and is rowed, as he related it to me, in a buffalo-hide boat to one of the islets.

Toward sunset he went down some steps to an underground corridor into which a series of grilles and doors opened, having in his brisk fashion already made a survey of the treasures above, and wishing to run over those below while there was still some twilight. Midway in the corridor, at a moment when, as it happened, the two monks were whispering together, he noticed a half-open grille, and passed in, whereat the grimmer of the two fellows stepped sharply up and tapped him on the shoulder, saying, "Not in there!" But Lepsius was already in, and making out that he didn't understand, took another step, and looked about him.

Three sides of this apartment were piled with papyri and many book-like objects dark with dust, together with pictures of saints all painted full-face, whatever the posture of the body, and with idols, weapons, beads, and other suchlike gems and curios. One wall of it, however, was almost bare, and there, in the centre of that wall, hung a little basalt stele, about as thick as one's wrist, and about six inches long; it had a copper cap with an old hole in it, through which passed the banyan string with which it was hung up. Lepsius could see that it was covered with a singular enough mixture of hieroglyphic, hieratic, and demotic figures; and his curiosity seems to have been at once fired to a high degree by this sight, especially when he saw marked on the wall over the stele in the Geez jargon the curious runes, "Riches of Jerusalem."

"Well," Lepsius said, "may I look about?" addressing himself to the milder of the two monks. The answer was, "No, it is the prior's room."

"And who is the dead man?" Lepsius asked.

"The prior," was the answer.

"Who died yesterday?"

"Yes."

"He died here, then?"

"Yes, in this chamber, where he mainly passed his time."

"Why did he pass his time here?" Lepsius wished to know.

"Because," was the answer, "he wanted to contemplate the sacred stele. For fifty years he was poring upon it, and dropped dead before it."

"Oho," says Lepsius, "and what is the history of the stele, my friend?"

"It fell from heaven," replied the monk; "the prior found it here when he was a very young monk, and hung it there under that picture of the Virgin, who was looking when he found it."

"Oho," says Lepsius, "but can't I approach a little and examine it?" The answer was, "No, the irreligious could not approach it."

"No one knows," was the answer.

"And yet you write over it, 'Riches of Jerusalem'?"

"Yes, for the prior discovered this much, that it tells of the riches of the City of God."

"He was a learned man, I see."

"We shall not have another like him! a learned and a saintly man. He made the stele the study of his life, and mined out much of its meaning, for which reason it is to be buried with him."

"Buried with him?" cries Lepsius.

"Yes, by his own instructions."

"And when?"

"To-night."

"Ah! At what hour?"

"At eleven."

"And where?"

"In the monastery."

But at this the more truculent of the two monks stepped offensively before Lepsius, blocking his view. The Galla warrior, too, who kept guard over the corpse was eyeing him disagreeably, so Lepsius moved off,

3

and after sauntering through another room or two, started off for the monastery-island, to be at once afresh drenched through by the rain. Darkness had suddenly come.

After a repast with the new prior, a portly man of middle age, he was conducted for the night to his chamber, where for a while he waited, sitting on a bed made of rushes mixed with raw cotton; but at ten o'clock he got up and stole through his door. Lepsius by this time had fully informed himself of the minutiæ of the dead prior's funeral, and had resolved to pilfer the little stele.

I think that I never knew quite so insolently plucky a nut as this of Lepsius. His impetuosity is extreme, and his tenacity is extreme; so that whatever happens at any time to fascinate his mind fascinates it in a quite unbalanced manner, to the banning of every other concern in the world. When this blessed stele had once seized upon his fancy as a thing likely to prove a scientific find, his subsequent action was so very in character, that I shouldn't wonder if he went stealing the thing, about to be buried and lost as it was, with an overweening sense of propriety, and perhaps, in setting about it, whispered to himself the word "Science," or perhaps only the word "Lepsius": I don't know.

But no man surely ever rushed into a job bristling with dangers more horrid, for he was alone among all those martial fanatics, and, save for a razor and a penknife, if I am right, quite unarmed.

He knew very well that he had only to be noticed prowling about in this way to set the whole place in a hullabaloo, and no doubt bring on his instant death; but the floors, covered with cocoanut-fibre, facilitated his flights and escapes, and he contrived to run the blockade to the landing-place. There his ears were aware of a priest baling rain-water from the boat meant to bring over the body of the prior, but so deep was the darkness of the night, that nothing could be seen a yard beyond one's eyes. With elaborate stealths Lepsius stepped down into a boat almost swamped with rain-water, put out the oar, and paddled off for the library-island.

His hope, derived from certain answers already given to his inquiries, was that the corpse might by this time be less closely guarded, that he might thus perchance be able to stretch a clandestine arm to the stele, and then, hastening back with it, steal into his chamber. But when with bare feet he had got down into the underground corridor of the stele and

4

corpse, and had peeped into the prior's room, there still lingered, brooding, the armed Galla. Lepsius was the last man alive to be baffled! He simply said to himself, "Well, the other way, then," went up afresh, towed his boat away from the landing-stage, sat down on a rock, and waited, his ear cocked to hear a sound through the showering of the rain.

The monks landed and entered the mosque.

After some twenty minutes they returned to the quay with rekindled torches, carrying the coffin: and though the largest of the boats was a craft as big as a Red Sea lugger, so overgrown was the size of the coffin, that they were obliged to lay it crosswise over the gunwales aft. Lepsius, himself unseen, could, by means of the flickering torch-lights, see all. He stole along the shore closer to the landing-stage. The placing of the coffin was a longish task; and out into darkness, one by one, cowered the lights, so that no more than two remained burning when the first of the boats pushed off, and the dirge was afresh lifted; and when at last all the boats were abroad on the water, the priests intoned in a complete darkness. Lepsius was then hanging to the transom of the boat which bore the coffin, she towing his length in her track.

Midway across, judging the moment come, he raised himself cautiously up; one stiff arm held up his weight on the transom, while with the other hand he groped, grasped the lid, tried to lift it. Lid wouldn't stir: it was fastened.

Another man might now, perhaps, have renounced the attempt, not knowing what string next to pull; it was in just such a plight that Lepsius was likely to show fight.

The man's a born theorist: would never dream of abandoning a conclusion based upon reasoning, because, perhaps, appearances should happen to combat it; and he had already reasoned that the lid was unnailed. He raised himself still further, felt with his hand over the surface of the lid, and was soon reassured, seeing that the priests, in order to keep the two pieces together during the passage, had tied two cords of banyan-twine bodily about lid and coffin; finding which, Lepsius dived into his pocket, took out a penknife, and cut the cords, deeming that the monks, when they saw the cords cut, the stele gone, would set it all down to a miracle of God. By this time the boats had floated the funeral-hymn pretty close up to the monks' home.

5

Lepsius splashed about, catching at the vacant air; but even in the very plight and fix of his death his reasoning mind was not drowned. He judged that he must now be very near the monastery, so that if he could find even a minute's support in the water, he might by such means manage some way to come at safety; but the boats had forged on well away beyond him, and there was no making out anything in that thickness of blackness. There was, however, one hope—the coffin: for, though he could not see, he knew perfectly the course of its sideward dive, and it was assuredly only the coffin, or the coffin-lid, which, if he was to find salvation, could save him. He quite well knew the science of swimming, though no master of the art: so, taking care to keep his lips closed, he made a few strokes, sinking and rising indeed, but moving, and his strokes proved in the duly right course, for very soon now he found himself on the coffin-lid, the little basalt stele hanging still to his forefinger by its string.

Lepsius scrambled up some rocks, and started slantways away from the throng of lights toward a wing of the building; and as the priests appear to have had no firearms, it became an affair of darting, Lepsius being a fairly nimble fellow, though, I fancy, without any wind to speak of, and already very weary. However, he reached the monastery-wall, and hastening along it, happened upon a small doorway, into which he darted, slammed the door, and was away anew through darkness; whereat the monks ran round to the front, and scattering there, rushed with rekindled torches in all directions through the monastery, scouring it for the fugitive.

Toward morning, it being still pitch dark, the Englishmen at Gondar who composed the mission were startled by the bombardment of the place set apart for their abode: for the priests and natives, failing to find Lepsius, had posted northward to seek vengeance upon the mission; whereat the British, in danger of their lives, were obliged to barricade their doors and defend themselves; and before the intervention of the *ras* was able to reach the residence, three Abyssinians were shot, so that this matter of the basalt stele had something of a grim beginning.

Not till six days later did Lepsius succeed in coming up secretly with his comrades, after seeing the lion and the hyrax, and a score of escapades; and on the sixteenth morning they all started eastward and coastward under an escort of the *ras*. The terror of the anger of England was, of course, extreme at the moment in the mind of the Negus and his Court, or it might have gone ill with Lepsius and his companions. However, all's well that ends well; nothing graver than threats came about, and Lepsius, having his basalt stele, could afford, I suppose, to grin his grin.

CHAPTER II.

MOLLY O'HARA.

PROFESSOR S. S. REID's history thus continues:

Well, I saw old Lepsius very shortly after his return, when he showed me the little cylinder of basalt, and related to me for the first time, not the last, the details of his adventures. He was blithe and fit, if a bit bothered in mind about the three shot Abyssinians, and about the drowning of the aged prior's body, due to his rage of research.

"And how about the stele," said I to him; "have you made out the meaning?"

"I am going to," was his answer.

"I suppose it is worth the pains?" said I.

"Reid," says he, "it would be worth the pains, if all the Orientalists in the world applied their wits to nothing else than that one thing."

"What makes you think that?" I asked.

Well, I wished him joy of his new toy, and we said adieu for that time.

Then for some few months I did not see much of Lepsius, nor, I imagine, did anyone else of his world, till his seclusion began to be remarked upon by one and another of the gossips. "Where was Lepsius, what was he pottering at at present, why the father of lies...?" and so on. On three or four of the occasions when I called upon him at his Hanover Square house, I found him looking far from so well and sprightly as usual, nor did the good fellow give himself the pains to hide from me that I was somewhat heavy upon him. I understood that he was in the grip of a fit of study—a certain grimness of his looks and gauntness of his face informed one of so much—and that in that same little stele lay the secret of this too great zeal. By this time the blessed stele had been reproduced and distributed among the savants everywhere, and it may be that a race was being run in its deciphering, I don't know; but one thing was obvious, it made Lepsius lean many days, so that says Matthews to me, "serves him right for picking and *steling*, there's some black spook in the basalt thing that's paying him back, and making him its victim"; and, in truth, I never saw such a thing, for one by one Lepsius threw every social, every scientific obligation to the winds to give himself day and night to this one object. Such, however, was the man: whatsoever his hands found to do, he did it with a fraction more than all his might or right. Then all at once I learned that he had fallen ill and had gone off to his castle in Galway, from which region, after some weeks, he once only wrote me a few words.

On a sudden one morning, say ten months after his coming back from Abyssinia, Lepsius presents his old phiz before me, looking as brisk and light as you like, with a smile on the thin lips. He had got back from Ireland only the day before, and, after some gossip, said I to him, "Come now, one can really see that we have laid bare at last the secret of our basalt stele."

"Do I look like it?" he asked rather sorrowfully.

"So I thought," said I.

"Just failed, sir! just failed!" sighs he, tossing up his hand.

"Tell me about it," said I.

"That's all I've got to say," says he; "I've only just failed. The epigraph, as you know, consists of signs of very diverse dates, with a quite hierogrammatic vowelling, but Memphitic aspirations, and a jumble of true idiographs and true rebuses. Well, within five months I had deciphered it all—every syllable—save fifteen signs, making, I think, three words at the very finish, which are purposely 'secret'; but, as it chances, those three are the important ones."

"That's hard luck, certainly," said I; "but why, then, are these three of such particular importance?"

"You know," said he, "that the stele is the record of an accumulation of riches heaped up somewhere by a host of Hindu princes during the period of the Mohammedan deluge—this where and when is exactly what remains dark. Fix place and date, and you have sextupled the value of your stele as a piece of history, quite apart from the pile of lucre in question, supposing it still to exist."

"Well, that's tantalising," I said. "Of course, Thibaut has seen it?"

"So much for stolen goods, then," said I. "Still, you seemed to me a good deal more like your old self just as you came in, quite a youthful step and jaunty air, I thought! so I made sure...."

He laughed, saying, "Well, perhaps you are right, for I *am* relieved, and I have reason."

"How do you mean?" I asked.

"Look you," says he, "I am going to read every syllable of the writing on that stele."

"You said just now that you couldn't," said I.

"I am going to, though," says he, "for it can be done, if not by me, if not by any living man, still it can be done; and if I look relieved it is because I know the means of doing it, and because, two nights since, lying in my bed, I suddenly decided to use them."

"Very good," said I, swallowing my puzzlement; "and what *are* the means?"

"I am going, Reid," says Lepsius, "to make a man who will read the secret."

Quite at a loss to make out what the deuce he would be at, no doubt I smiled, for he added quickly, "No, don't smile in that fashion, as if you hadn't known me until to-day, since I assure you quite seriously that I can and will successfully accomplish this job."

"The making of a man?" said I: "those are your words."

"The making of a man," says he, "who will not merely read the rebus, but do it without difficulty—without effort."

"Lord," exclaims Lepsius, "what a speech! How sweet the smile, but how icy the meaning! as if I were some rash, fantastic talker. No! at present I haven't the time to go into prolonged explanations, moreover doubting Thomas ought to be tortured; but in about four days I shall probably lay my plan fully before you, when I shall have seen the initial stages of it well under way: and meanwhile, I invite you to take part with me in watching the accomplishment of these stages."

"Where?" said I.

"You come," said he.

"To the end of the world," said I, "if you are serious and scientific."

"I am quite serious and strictly scientific," says he.

"There, I think," he says, "comes the right age, the right race, the right trade, the right body and being—the very lady."

It was a passing woman at whom he pointed, a woman of the lower orders, with black hair, black eyes, high cheek-bones, very cheaply dressed, but not unclean, long in the leg, lean and fit, some twenty-five years old. Her nose was not red, her teeth were regular. She was going, under a heap of soiled clothes, toward the Surrey side, and one could make quite sure that she was an Irish washerwoman.

Well, Lepsius stepped out and addressed the woman. She was startled! I heard her say, "Sure, then, it isn't me that has the time to be showing your worship around the town this day."

I remained waiting at the parapet, absolutely astonished, much amused, while Lepsius walked on with the woman, talking pressingly, quite a confab, one could see, taking place between them, he all suave insistence, the woman curtseying, till, presently turning, he beckons me to come. So I ran and overtook them, to find them already fast friends; and Lepsius effusively introduced me to "Miss Molly O'Hara."

This woman turned out to be the heartiest, best soul in the world, and in some half-hour we had won from her the whole simple history of one who was orphaned and friendless, save for a sister, a fruit-seller, who lived at Ballihooly. In the course of our discourse it was discovered that she had never visited the Tower, the Crown Jewels, nor the whispering-gallery at St. Paul's, so we soon got from her an engagement to meet us on the Bridge the next day, in order to go with us to inspect these glories. She showed us the slum and the house in Southwark in which she occupied a room, and we parted.

Well then, the next day, at one o'clock, behold Molly standing in holiday garb with her landlady for guardian, and the pair of professors before them with doffed hats, like characters in an opera! We had lunch in a restaurant, and I spent a pestilent day in the "chamber of horrors" and other suchlike places, winding up with a play in the evening; after which, at about midnight, we sent our ladies home in a cab, and Lepsius, coming back to my house with me, disclosed to me that night the design that underlay his conduct during the last two days, so that we were still talking in my study when the dawn stole in. When I said to him that I had well earned his secret, and asked what in the world he meant to do with this Molly O'Hara, his answer was, "I mean to make her read my stele for me." "Quite so," said I, "but then, Lepsius, you persist in speaking to me in riddles." "I mean to marry her," says Lepsius.

I was so startled, I couldn't help crying out a "No!"

"And why not?" says the doctor coldly.

11

"Oh, Lepsius," I couldn't help saying, half laughing, and half shrinking with reproach, "this is ridiculous, this is absurd."

"Ridiculous enough, certainly," says he, "but very far from absurd. We differ there."

"But, Lepsius," said I.

"Pooh, man," says he, "don't be excessive; there's no law to prevent me taking a female to the altar, if I like, and, as to the particular lass in question, if it isn't the right of men like you and me to look at facts in their true light, where's the use of us? Molly O'Hara is a better human being than I, you may bet, with all my learning, sound from her top-knot to her toes; I don't doubt she will make a pretty fairish wife—and a most splendid mother."

"Well, I never was so astonished," I said.

"That," he answered, "is due to the fact that you have not yet acquired a scientific interest in my motive, for as soon as ever you have, your interest will quite quash your astonishment."

"Well, I am all ears," says I: "what *is* your motive?"

"I see," said I: "given fair materials to start with, you undertake what you say."

"Aye," says he, "and without so much as the shadow of a doubt as to the result."

"What an enterprise!" I cried. "But as to the means."

"The means," says he, "will be simple enough, being based purely upon the known fact that human beings are what their environment makes of them. We know that an English child, abandoned by its guardians in China, will grow up, hardly a mental Englishman, but a mental Chinaman: never by any effort will he be able to row like a Cambridge-man, or do business like a jobber; but he will, without effort, make finer porcelain than could be turned out by the life's devotion of ten thousand Cambridge-men or jobbers; it is a question of environment, of the mental hue and house about you. Be sure that every brat born into ancient Athens was straightway an artist, and if children to-day were born into a world in which everybody as a matter of course played violins with perfect skill, then *every* average child would without conscious effort be a pretty perfect fiddle-player—and, indeed, *is* so in some regions of the Bas-Pyrennees. It is a question of environment."

"Quite so," said I, "and, if you add heredity——"

"Quite so," said I; "one has no difficulty in following you so far, for even monkeys that have lived long in an environment of men become manlike, and get to do many things; so, given your 'environment of gods,' your undertaking looks all in bloom. But where, then, do you mean to find this environment of gods? On the moon? In Venus?"

"Oh, as to that," says Lepsius, "surely that much is simplicity itself. The environment may be real or it may be merely imagined. A child placed in isolation may be made to believe in an environment, a world, which does not exist, and so long as he never comes into actual contact with the imperfect world, and has no suspicion that it is not a perfect one, you will have all the elements of success: his life-ideal and standard, his idea and atmosphere, will remain quite unaffected by the actual world round about him; and having been made to conceive man as a god, he will not himself be vastly inferior to his conception."

"By George," I cried, "I see what you are at!... But, my friend, aren't you preparing a nice little shock for some poor devil of a child, supposing he ever does come into contact with his actual, as distinct from his fancied, environment?"

"May be," says Lepsius, with a shrug; "or may be the shock will be to the environment, not to the child—'so much the worse for the coo,' as old Stephenson said; but really, Reid, that's looking too far forward for me; the practical point for us is to make out the meaning of our stele.... Lord! it is broad day, I'm away."

Such is something of the gist of my talk with this radical mind that morning. I can't recall a hundredth part of his ratiocinations, but when he had finished I was convinced. I made him stay till with our own hands we had found and cooked some coffee on my tripod, whereupon the doctor went home.

CHAPTER III.

THE ISLE OF LIES.

If what has so far been given by Professor Reid be read as a sort of prologue, nearly nineteen years may well be passed over in silence, till, patching artfully into one a number of letters of Dr. Lepsius to the professor, we watch what then befell. The doctor writes:

My friend, it was just on his nineteenth birthday, the 21st of July, that, strange to say, it was to happen; the day which I had long determined in my own mind as that on which I should present him the little stele to read.

Well then, aware that he is below waiting, I pull myself together now, put a bit of go into my gait and glance, and down I go to him; together we stand at the gate of our little home—alas, for the last time—my grey head reaching little higher than his shoulder, Reid, for the old spine bows a bit now, you know; and from the kitchen Shan Healy looks up to watch the race for the thousandth time, while away in the west the sun is going down all in a wild of clouds and glories, as often in this wet place. The sea is dead, just lapping the beach in a weary way; the sky grey, with a curlew or two skirling under it. It gives a little relief to live it over again....

There then, we stand, ready to renew the old, old trial of thews. You know that it has ever been my policy to speak as few words as possible to this creature, so now I only say to him, "Well, ready?"

"Ready, sir," answers my man.

"Then one, two—*Three!*"

Darkness was beginning to fall rapidly, the winds to pipe up a bit, as he and I together strolled back homeward in silence all over the western shores, upon which the waters were just moving themselves to moan and spume. I willed it so always, for along the eastern shores, where I was believed to have passed, there was ever a certain absence of foot-prints! And Mr. Hannibal often seemed to have the knack of seeing in the dark.

Have I done well? Have I done right? Never did a question of that sort arise in my mind till within the twelve months gone, when I have had to ask myself, "Have I, who forgot nothing, forgotten one thing—one thing needful?" God Almighty forgive His faulty ones. I am an old man now, with the back bowing down, and a head of white hairs, meekly aware of my own weaknesses and achings....

Sometimes lately, Reid, I may avow to you, I have stolen out of my room in the dead of night and stood before his door, stood for hours, hearkening for a sound; couldn't at all tell you why—bound there somehow—and I have shaken my poor head, saying to myself, "No, surely, I have to cure myself of this folly: a purely scientific interest in this savage, nothing more"; but still I have stuck at his door.

But to return to this birthday-eve of his. We two had made our way back together in silence, nearly to the castle-gate, when out darts Shan Healy, wringing hands and crying, "Oh, Master Hannibal, do forgive me, sir, the glass pot has boiled all over, while I was attending to the dinner"; whereat Master Hannibal, without waiting to hear another word, threw Shan out of his way, and rushed into the house, no doubt to see for himself how the matter stood, for he seems to have left some mess simmering in his laboratory, had bid Shan look to it, and the thing had had some mischance.

"Now, here's a go for a poor chap, doctor," says Shan to me, in great distress; "believe me, I couldn't avoid it, the thing boiled over so quick, and what'll Master Hannibal say now?"

"Say?" said I, for I was angry, "what can he dare say? Let him go to the devil, you couldn't help it, and I order you not to distress yourself in the slightest."

"Ah, doctor, it's all very well for you to talk," says he.

Beside myself with anger, I pounded upon the door, and now at once the row stopped, and in a moment Shan opened, saying despondently to me, poor chap, "Oh, doctor, he do use me cruel, sir, cruel, cruel, cruel. Oh, my poor head—what does he think anybody is made of?"

My own head was hung with shame; I could do nothing but silently pat my old companion on his shoulder.

"Where is he now?" said I.

"Gone like a shadow through the window, doctor, and down to the shore, the minute he heard you pounding," says Shan. "He held me down on the floor with one hand, and with the other he banged my poor head ... cruel, cruel. I shouldn't mind if it was done in a rage, but smiling as cool as a cucumber, as if anybody's head was a block of wood he was playing with."

"Well," I said bitterly, "all your own fault, Shan Healy; you're too faithful and good." And I left him there and went up.

CHAPTER IV.

THE SHIP.

The morning after, his birthday, on meeting him at the breakfast-table as the clock struck eight, I observed to him that he couldn't have had much sleep: to which, glancing up from his book, he answered, "Enough for the needs of my nature, sir, I think, though I was at work at four minutes before five. The old have greater need of repose, it appears, while, as to the young, the demagogue Cataline, it is written, could dispense with sleep almost altogether."

"Oho," said I; "well, let us be eating," and we sat to the old jug of porridge and oaten loaf.

Presently, as we ate, I said to him, "By the way, I want you now to understand that you are not to knock my servant's head about any more."

His answer was that he had discovered that such occasional visitations had the effect of slightly heightening the functioning of the idiot's wit.

"Never mind your discoveries," said I: "you are not to do it, sir."

"I will not, sir," says he with his formal bow, and buries his brow anew in his volume.

"True, sir," says my man, "you did speak to me on this subject on the third of June two years ago, but your words did not give me an impression of great urgency, so I have dared to disregard them, since, after all, the digestion of the young is hearty and strong, and the days are hardly born but they are fled, and it is hard to the foot to race after the fastness of the horses of time; hence the greater masters, the minds of white-hot ardour, like Cæsar, always delighted themselves in the most entangled exercises, like the dictating of a vast host of letters at once, so as to harbour in their mood a habit of keeping pace with the fleetness of the passing days."

"So true," said I, "so true; still, it is as well not to eat and read together; nor are you any longer so 'young' as you have been; you know, of course, that to-day is your birthday."

"So I calculate, sir," says he: "I have now existed apart from the womb nineteen times as many as three hundred and sixty-five days, less four; that is to say, six thousand nine hundred and thirty-one days, without counting some odd hours."

"Oho," said I; "and how are you going to spend the day?"

"I am engaged in a chemical investigation, sir," says he, leaning back now, and balancing a plate on the edge of his forefinger nail, for he always speedily devoured his food, though with complete mastication, I believe, and was generally done before I was nearly through.

"Ah, and what is the investigation?" I asked.

"You must have noticed, sir," says he, "the agitation I call it, with which bismuth acts——"

"I know exactly what you are going to say," said I—God forgive us—"quite so; but look here, before you go I want to show you something, something that will amuse you; just read me that."

On a sudden now, Reid, the moment long waited for had come, for I now caught the old basalt stele out of my pocket, and laid it before him; whereat immediately the fellow seemed to feel an interest in the mere sight of this object, took it up, looked it up and down and round about, smiling his smile, his brow twitching into momentary frowns.

"Why, sir," says he suddenly, "where did you come upon this stone?"

"That's not the point," said I; "I got it in Abyssinia, but that's not the point; just read it."

"It is mainly enchorial and alphabetic," he breathes aloud, peering into the thing, "but with a great number of syllabary signs, and vowel matres lectionis——"

"Yes, I know; read it," said I, painfully conscious within myself of being pale in the face.

"Strange," says he to himself: "both Sahidic and Memphitic, but mainly Memphitic——"

"Yes, I tell you, I know," said I; "read it, read it, boy."

He hesitated, sir, and I felt growing within me an agitation almost too great to be any more restrained.

"Have *you* read it, sir?" he suddenly asks, raising his eyes to my face; and I was foolishly conscious that my eyes drooped before his, even as in a tone of protest I answered, "Why, naturally! I only give it to you as a little exercise to amuse you; just read the whole thing right off."

Now, sir, he puts the bit of a stele on the table, and he bends his brow studiously over it, supporting his head between his hands.

"Seven of the words are purposely secret," says he to himself; "it is not an easy cypher...."

"Well, I know, I know that," said I, deadly anxious now, "that's why I give it to you—for a little fun on your birthday; just read it off, boy, to please me."

"Ah, I see," says he all at once: "this whole half-line is a long rebus or pun; the sound of each ideograph combines with the third following to form a word: that is clearly the idea of the inventor; I can trace his thought; I see. Oh, it is not difficult, sir!"

"Good—very good," said I; "then just read it right off, and go up to your science, boy," for I felt my face growing white with excitement, see-ing that, in spite of his brave words, the man's manner showed some hes-itation, and lower and lower bent his head over the thing.

"A moment, sir," he murmurs, "one moment; your servant is slow and dull, but"—something; and another minute went by in a silence that was most bitter to me to bear, till, all in a scare, I called to him, "Well, but haven't you done it *yet*?"

"Yes, sir, I think——" he falters.

"Then read it!"

"In Coptic?"

"In English."

There my man stopped short. "At," he repeated, but couldn't go on, and there in the shameful silence he sat now frowning into the thing with a sort of haughty, excruciated self-surprise, but without progress.

"Well?" said I, and my looks, I know, were ghastly, for all that he had read of the thing I, too, long ago had read, though I admit that it had cost me some few months of effort.

"At, sir," says he, more to himself than to me, "at—something; fifteen other ideographs remain, making three words, I am certain. But they are without determinatives, and their outlines are so blurred, they bring no meaning, no meaning—to my mind; they seem to belong...."

"Better say at once, Hannibal, that you can't read the epigraph!" I cried out.

"*You* have read it, sir, no doubt?" says he for the second time with, I fancied now, just a touch of scepticism somewhere.

"Why, naturally, boy!" I cried, with such a noise that, at the moment, I almost believed it myself. "Can't *you*, then?"

"It is strange, sir," says he, "it seems to contain *htar*, and the old verb *secha*, to write.... Pray, bear with your servant a little, sir, I shall read the words, I see clearly that I *can*, if you will only vouchsafe me a little time—down by the seashore."

CHAPTER V.

"MISS EVE."

At this point the statement of Dr. Lepsius becoming devoid of interest for us, we may next take up that of one Jeanne Auvache, where she writes (in French, with no eye to *us*, but quite for her own behoof):

* * * *

"Little that imports to me, your name," said I: "I wish to know, since you are not one of the ship's company, how came you here?"

His answer was a whisper at my ear that I already broke my vow, since I spoke loudly enough, he said, to be heard by everyone throughout the vessel; but that since he was now certain that he was more powerful than I, therefore he would throw me down, and bind me anew, if I betrayed him "to Man."

As I said this, my young man, without saying more, drops on a sudden down, with his hands outstretched to me: and when I said to him, "Well, what now?" his answer was a prayer not to be untrue to him, but to hide him "from Man" and be his wife!

I laughed anew at this within myself! for he seemed to be blind to my forty-one foundered summers, and the flowers that withered in them, he a youth of hardly twenty years. So I said to him, "Get away with you, for you are crazy; how do you know that I am not already a married woman with a husband?" on which he told me very secretly that in any case he believed it to be possible that he should be able to make me one of "the most sovereign of ladies," and with that he presents me with a piece of stone, resembling an ink-bottle, saying to me, "Read that."

"I know nothing of this," said I to him, handing him back the piece of stone, whereat he peered piercingly at me a moment, and then all at once a light seemed to dawn upon his mind, and he rose up from his knees saying to himself, "I thought so."

"Thought what?" said I to him, but to this he made no reply, only smiled upon me.

He gave me an impression of some young god gone mad! "You are hardly very polite," I said to him, "and another woman might think you a little crazed, since at one moment you crave to be my husband, and at

21

another moment you smile upon me as upon some ninny," to which he replied something about being bound to adore me, ninny or no, inasmuch as I am so adorable!

"Why, get you gone," I said to him, "you have hardly had time to see me yet!"

He asked me how much time was necessary, and if he had not gazed at me through the bushes?

"Those, then, were your eyes that gazed there at Shunter through the bushes at me?" said I; "and you found me beautiful? What, then, could you have found so very beautiful about me, my face, or my figure—or both?" to which he replied, "Both."

"And do you mean," said I to him, "that it was merely through love of me that you concealed yourself in the yacht? What a sudden flame of passion! But I am at a loss to know how you could come here!" on which he explained that he had swum under water from the shore.

"But how could you possibly steal down here without being seen?" I asked him, to which he replied that "that question of itself charged me with a drowsy consciousness."

His little smile of a superior man (*petit sourire d'homme supérieur*)! "Well," said I fondly to him, "you, for your part, are of a wakeful consciousness, and I, for mine, am beautiful both in face and form, is it not so? and it is a pair of us, is it not? But since we are now about to come to land, tell me this——" but before I could utter another word I heard the call of "Jeanne," and was recalled by it to this world. It was the voice of Miss Eve who called me, and ere I could find my tongue to reply she called again, "Jeanne, where are you?" but I could not answer her, my eyes were fixed upon the boy, who now appeared lost in a joyous attention to the call, and with his finger held up gave deep into my ear a whisper of "Sweet voice." Whereat I, being a little perturbed, turned from him, switched off the light, whispered him to await my return there, and went out in haste to Miss Eve, wondering within myself how in Heaven's name I was now to restrain him from making the acquaintance of other ladies.

CHAPTER VI.

THE TOWERS.

I now went into the question of our wedding, telling him how everything could be fixed up in some days, how I found myself possessed of two hundred pounds funded out of my earnings, which amount would serve nicely for our small *ménage*, till he should have found his niche in the world; and I engaged myself to see to everything as to getting the licence from the surrogate, as I desired him meanwhile to hide in the church-steeple near St. Peter, whither twice a day I would fetch him a meal: for I did not wish him to see the world at all as yet, and so, working on his awes as to his father, I warned him that he would certainly be caught, if he but once looked forth of his hiding; though, *after* our marriage, I said, he could safely range out anywhere, since the laws would not allow his father to take him out of his spouse's arms.

CHAPTER VII.

THE TERRACES.

Arrived at The Towers, I first slumbered a couple of hours, and then, the day still early, returned to my mistress' bedside. She had bidden me wake her, but I just massaged her with a gentle touch, contemplating with a smile of pleasure that face whose charms I am soon no more to behold: and never did she show to me in so angel-like a light as then, for everything is suddenly changed in me, I find myself inclined to be kindly-minded to everybody, and then Miss Eve is ever beguiling, from her very breathing being given forth a breeze fraught with that fainting fragrance of frangipane, which is as essentially a part of her self as are her eyes or her smile. When her lids unclosed of their own action she once more bathed, and it was when I was doing her hands in making her toilette for the forenoon that she begged me to bear tea with my own hands to her, if she should happen to be in the small drawing-room after four that afternoon.

I crept then through the bushes of the lake's edge, till I came to the lawn; and there, observing their backs turned toward me, I stalked still further forward on my hands and knees, till I was in concealment beneath the stonework of a terrace—little dreaming that I had been overheard; and thence I heard the voice of Miss Ruth saying to the boy, "But you must have lived in a strange isolation never to have heard speak of Jesus Christ?" upon which he, gazing down upon the ground, said in a low tone that he was altogether ignorant, till two days ago having never met with anyone save his father and an idiot.

"Poor dear boy!" coos the voice of Miss Ruth, who, being but twenty-five years of age, has scarcely the right, I think, thus to soothe a youth of twenty. "And where," says she, "was this?"

In a tone in his throat he replied, "On an island of the Outer Hebrides."

"Why, I am even now from there!" she told him. "But your father, has he also never known the blessed name of Jesus?"

He answered her that his father possesses the sum of worldly wisdom, but that he had never at all heard from his father any mention of this personage.

To this he answered that he had never heard these words.

"Tell me this, then," said she: "in what year is it that we are now living?" to which he made her the amazing answer that we are now in the year six hundred thousand three hundred and sixty-three.

At this reply Miss Ruth smiled, and during some time appeared wrapped in silent prayer, until she suddenly asked him, "From what event, then, do you date this vast sum of years?"

"From the presumed date of the evolution of human life from the ape-state," was his reply.

For a few moments Miss Ruth mused upon the young man, then threw up her hands with drollery in her little human way which just rescues her from being angelic; and she asked him, "But are not all dates reckoned among us from the Lord Christ?"

At these words of hers he seemed extremely perplexed, and, after frowning upon the ground, asked her if the Lord Jesus Christ was a Greek or a Roman.

"He was a Hebrew!" cries Miss Ruth.

"With an Arianised name," said he: "lived, then, under the later Romans."

"Just so," said she: "how much you know for one of your station, and how little!"

Miss Eve had as yet uttered not a word, but now with her eyes turned downward, her lips muttered, "Why, yes."

He smiled, and at the same time looked perfectly perplexed, turning his stare from one to the other lady, until Miss Ruth remarked to him, "Do not doubt it, though it is marvellous in all our eyes, so that even the cherubic natures of the skies deeply brood with admiration upon it," and he then very impolitely replied to her that her consciousness of the size of this earth could not be alert.

To this answered Miss Ruth, "The earth? she is huge in momentousness, you know: with each tick of the clock a human being ceases to breathe——"

"A human being?" he replied with a cry of surprise: "with each tick of the clock a million worlds are burned, and are born!"

"Oh, La!" says she, startled a little at him.

Then she said, with that veiling of the eyes with the eyelids that lends her her air of Madonna saintliness, "That cannot be, I think."

But the other sister murmured, "Ruth, it must truly be so, if the universe truly is termless: prove me one world that's been burned, millions a minute must burn."

"Let it be so, then," said Miss Ruth, "since you say so, and glory be to God, for the remotest of them, I think, His hand holds, and His right hand guides it."

"He is it," the young man said.

"He is with it, I think," Miss Ruth replied.

"And *you* also say this?" he asked of Miss Eve.

"Yes," she answered curtly, with a touch of pique, as it appeared to me.

Silent he stood now a while, with that smile of his that hides all the windings of his mind behind his brow, but still giving an impression of one plunged in bewilderment at the creatures he was speaking with. Then, glancing upward, he swept his fingers athwart the vault of the stars, with the remark that all that was a darksome mathematic, a perfection which was deaf.

The two ladies looked round, and "which 'fourth sharer' can he mean?" Miss Ruth wished to know of Miss Eve, while I crouched there beneath the terrace, trembling lest he should betray my whereabouts; but when they pressed him to say where I was, to my great gladness, he gave an evasive reply.

He next requested Miss Ruth to instruct him further in her views of the universe, upon which she begged him to come the next night that she might give him a Bible and teach him of the Lord Jesus; and as to his father, after some hesitation on her part, he gained from her a promise that, if his father, or his father's agents, should get upon his scent, the sisters would not let out to them where he lurked down there in the river-cave. And next he began to beg Miss Eve for one of the begonias at her girdle, but at that moment, before he could be answered, Monsieur le Comte de Courcy stepped out of the house, and, really as if by magic, the instant he appeared the young man had vanished. By this time I had somewhat recovered of my fit of affright, my eyes were anew at the parapet-top, and I could spy the surprise of the ladies, who seemed unable to believe what their two eyes had seen: for though the nearest leafage was quite nineteen or twenty metres away, in the twinkling of an eye, as it seemed, he was within it, and gone like a ghost at cock-crow.

I, for my part, having crawled back to the lake, rushed through the shrubbery obliquely, meaning to meet him somewhere in his career downward: but he was nowhere to be found, until I was on the footpath above the cliffs, when down there in the moonlight I beheld him walking furiously to and fro before his cave's mouth. Down, then, I scrambled, calling out to him, asking why he had not awaited me; but he is not very well-bred, went on silently walking, and on marking one of the swans glide past on the water, he suddenly darted to lie on his face and gaze at it.

"But why did you fly like that?" I asked him when he returned to me, "since the gentleman could not have hurt you?" but still he made me no reply.

"And what did you think of the two ladies?" I next asked him.

Then he: "Who are those ladies?"

I: "They are Miss Ruth and Miss Eve Vickery, the daughters of Mr. Richard Vickery, who is what is called 'An Iron King,' a very rich and an extremely religious man, who sometimes preaches in a chapel on Sundays."

He: "Preaches?"—and I had now to try to explain that "preaching" means teaching the people how to be devout and grave; but I failed to get him to comprehend how Mr. Vickery could have attained to greater gravity than the rest, and he struck his brow in the misery of his failure to grasp the signification of a single word that I uttered as to this. "Well, it is so, and that is all," I said at last; "but as to the ladies, you have still not told me which of the two you most admire."

Then he: "Which is the first-born?"

He: "A saint?"—and I had anew to make an explanation which he little comprehended, and then anew I wished to know of him which of the two sisters he the most admired.

And now he, making that stone like an ink-bottle which he keeps inside his shirt whirl about his forefinger without attachment in a quite wonderful way, his waist swaying to keep the thing whirling wildly quick, answered with whistling lips, "I like Miss Ruth."

Then I: "Oh, you do? You like her better, I see, than you do Miss Eve?" upon which he, putting his hand behind his back for the stone to whirl behind there, answered, "Yes."

Then I: "But leaving Miss Ruth out of the question, since she will never marry, which of the two do you most admire—Miss Eve or me?"

He: "You."

I: "Oh, you do?"

He whistled quietly awhile, whirling the thing wildly with a swaying waist, as it were a wheel wheeling on his hand, and he answered, "Yes" to me; but I thought that my heart would be breaking with its rankling.

So I: "She has promised, yes, but she little means it, wait, you will see, you little know women, they are deceivers all; she will betray you surely enough, if she but has the chance."

He glanced sharply at me, then said, "No."

I: "But I say yes."

He: "The lapwing says pee-wit."

What he meant I was not sure, but I was so broken-hearted that night, that with sobs I threw myself now in a passion to his breast, and on my knees, kissing my own tears on his hands, implored him like a dear boy not to leave and despoil me, but to love me for ever, for if he left me, that would be my death, I said, and his death as well.

He smiled with his fixed little smile upon me, and I could believe that he meant well by me; so, getting up now, I told him how I had that day gained all information as to English marriages, and meant on the morrow to take the first measures; but as I was speaking of this, he, leaning aside, bent his ear to the ground, hearing God only knows what sound under the grass, and when I had bidden him good-night, and was going up the cliff's brow again, on glancing back I beheld him bent down aside, eagerly listening with his ear near the ground.

CHAPTER VIII.

IN THE GARDEN.

The next day the first thing that happened was the coming of a person whom Miss Ruth interviewed for her father in the morning-room. I was even then seeking Miss Ruth for Miss Eve, and on coming near the room could hear the man say that he was one Shan Healy, a servant of Dr. Lepsius, who, having traced to The Towers the owners of the yacht which had touched at Shunter, was now come to find out what he could as to his master's son.

He seemed a person of some thirty years, slimly tall, with a scar that twists his upper lip, clad in rough new clothes: a man of an alert and amiable personality, so that Miss Ruth laid her hand on his sleeve to soothe him, for indeed he was in deep dreariness, and frequently sniffled. When I went in with the message, Miss Ruth sent me to call Miss Eve to her, so I ran back, and having brought Miss Eve, hung near to hear.

Now Miss Eve knit her brows, and presently replied, "Promises can't be repealed, dear."

"But since it may do much harm?" Miss Ruth suggested.

"Still," muttered the lips of Miss Eve, "a promise."

"Oh, lady, do, for God's sake," Healy now entreated of Miss Ruth, "not that I expect him to go back with me, but he's so green to everything, badly needs somebody, lady, like a whale run ashore, has got no razors to shave, no jacket——"

At this of "razors," Miss Ruth placed her hand upon the man's in a movement of friendliness: for in truth he appears to be rather like his young master's nurse than servant, and Miss Ruth's heart, like waters haunted with squalls, is anew every minute smitten with all the world's smart, as fluid and easy as Miss Eve is aloof. So she smiles with the man, saying, "Wait, I'll question my God," and gets up to go away to a window, from which she presently returns to Miss Eve with the words, "Eve, I'll peach."

To this Miss Eve at first answered nothing, but after a little asked, "What will he think of the worth of the promises made by us Christians? Knowing a first that has failed, never a second he'll trust"; but Miss Ruth continued to believe that it would be better on the whole to betray; did not, however, outright do so, only revealing to Healy that the boy would be coming that evening to receive a Bible, and instructing Healy to be then on the terraces to meet him.

For the evening Miss Eve, for some reason, would put on her poudre blue with the Borzoi ornaments, and orchids, and now I had a small hour to myself, for, as to dinner, eating was far enough beneath that sphere of fairies where my brain was in a reel; so, having merely tasted a spoonful of soup, off I hastened to him....

He was not there at the cave, still he was not there! And I could only guess that, his awes of his "Man" having already grown less great, he had roamed far, and ah, I asked my heart if he had not done it four days too soon for my fate.... I had no paper to write him that he would be betrayed by the ladies if he came up, and after half an hour's waiting returned to The Towers.

Nothing was then left me to do but to watch, and at first I lurked under the conservatory's shadow, and then, conscious that I might be observed, moved up to pry from behind the curtains of that front bedroom on the right.

"Really?" says Miss Ruth to him, "and what, sir, is the name of this poor man who was burnt?" to which he gave the answer that he had heard the man called "George Perkins, the grocer."

"What, Mr. Perkins, the grocer, of Up Brooming?" cries Miss Ruth shrinkingly, with eyes of alarm, "burnt to death?" and "Oh!" she murmured with ruth.

To this he replied—and I disliked him for it—that there was no need for any feeling of grief or loss, since this grocer's life, he felt certain, was a life of no value, one greatly below the human grade, his figure having the grossness of the gorilla's, and his soul on a similar level, since in the attempt that he had made to steal he had failed even to death....

"To steal?" breathed Miss Ruth; "Mr. Perkins, the grocer? A prayer-leader? There must be some mistake!"

"No," he said—at least he took it, he said, for granted that the grocer had meant to steal, since there appeared to be no other motive for his demented rush into the conflagration.

"He rushed to rescue the child!" cries Miss Ruth.

CHAPTER IX.

"VITRIOLISERAI."

The next morning he was gone, he was not there in the cave, and as for the man, Healy, he was not there, and where to seek I knew not at all: only the thing like a telescope was there in the cave, the thing like a trap, the dead creature's remains, the stone which he has hollowed into a vase, and under some rubbish and leaves in a corner the thing like an ink-bottle that he has called a "stele": but all the bread, etc., that I had brought him he had either eaten or taken away.

Eaten, may be; but, if not eaten, whither, I asked myself—with this food—was he off to? Ah, many questions I asked myself; and then, hurrying across the bridge, went to the cottage of Mrs. Bream, with whom Healy was lodging, to ask if the man did not sleep there the previous night; but she said no, he had merely come in, together with a stripling who wore sandals, to take away his bag, saying, however, that he would be back to her in some days; and he had taken the 10.20 up-train with this stripling, who had wished to know of her, poor sinner, if she did not know even so much as the names of the mountains in the moon.

The 27th. But is he such a blackguard, or is his scorn of me so great, that he cannot even write me a line to say that I am never again to see him? Still not even a line, and Miss Eve this morning would not let me do her hands, but ordered me to bed, I looked so bad. I went, but had to get up to go to St. Arvens to receive the marriage-licence, after which I took the train, as directed, to Wynton, to give notice of it to the registrar there; and now any day after to-morrow, this gentleman told me, I may be married: a statement that made me in coming down the stairs break bitterly out into tears.... In passing through Wynton I procured myself at the chemist's a vial of vitriol....

The 29th. Well, dear Lord, he is here, and I thank you. I now write at six in the morning, after having spent a nearly sleepless night with him and Healy, and still with no desire to close my eyes. By to-morrow evening we shall have been secretly and safely married, and within a week I shall have taken farewell of this my life here....

I was in the housekeeper's room alone, for Mrs. Bowden had gone up, it being long past midnight, and I was lying on the sofa, the vial of vitriol beside me on the table, for I had been foolishly fingering it, when there came a tapping at that back door which opens upon the passage. I get up, I go to it, I open it.... And it was *he*! Oh, my wild one with wings, with the light of life flying wildly in his eyes, it was he! and while one might reckon three I stood breathless, then with a cry was on his breast.

His nature is not yet coaxed over into tolerating the luxury of kissing, and even in the ecstasy of our meeting his chastity shrank from the touch of my lips; but, my faith, that will soon be "al-right"! and he patted my shoulder fondly, even while hurriedly saying, "I need light for an hour or two."

I was too much flurried to attend to what he said! I cooed to him, "And is it actually true that you have come back to me?"

"Yes, yes, let me get in," he mutters hurriedly, and now, seizing Healy by the sleeve, hurries in into the housekeeper's room. He had climbed outside, and spied me alone in there through the window, Healy told me afterwards.

"But tell me——" I began to say to him, when "*Sh-h-h!*" breathes Healy into my ear, "*I'*ll tell you," and draws me away to a corner, where he whispers me, "Mum, can you offer a body such a thing as a bite of something? He"—indicating Hannibal Lepsius with his thumb—"can do without food and sleep, but that's a bit more than *I* can bring off, anyway."

I made him sit, stole out, and in five minutes was back with bread, meat, cheese, and a bottle of beer. Hannibal Lepsius at this time could no more be said to be sitting, but was half over the table, one knee on the chair, poring with greed over that "stele," as if he would eat it with his gaze. I was about to say something to him, when my ear was afresh reached by the *sh-h-h* of Healy, like a whispering of leafage fretted by a zephyr; so I placed the victuals on Healy's knees, sat before him, and commenced to question him; but it was many minutes before his stuffed mouth could bring out a syllable.

"Why were you so famished?" I asked him, "since you had money to pay railway-fare?"

With his lips at my ear, he answered: "It was a question of time, mum—no time to eat, no time to sleep; but that's good meat, that is, and that's good beer, too."

"Was he, then, in such a hurry to return to his marriage?" I asked.

32

The man looked at me under his eyes—strangely, I thought—and replied, "I know nothing of that, mum; but we went to see London, and we saw it in a tear, I tell you, and we left it in a tear, for by the end of the third day London had got a bit too hot for us."

"Why, how was that?" I asked him.

"Truth is," he whispered, "some of us have been putting into our pockets more than what belongs to us!"

"What!" I said.

"*Sh-h-h,*" he went.

Mrs. Bowden's clock just then struck one, and glancing round at it, I beheld Hannibal Lepsius bent yet further over the table, poring upon that stone, and heard him whimper over it as if in pain.

"What is he doing?" I whispered to Healy.

"Lord knows, mum," he whispered back.

"So the London police were after him?"

"That's so."

"What a thing!" I said in awe.

"Thrice in three days!" he whispered; "aye, and that second time it was a close go with us, too, seeing that he wouldn't let go hold of me—a thousand people after us through London streets, if there was one, and he dragging me, thinking that I am against him, too, and want to betray him. That's hard, too, that's hard. Here am I, mum, Dr. Lepsius' servant—I'd give this hand for the doctor—yet keeping the lad dark from the doctor, going against the doctor, mind, knowing that I am doing wrong, but no more able to help it than a man addicted to liquor, I am that given up to the lad; yet he keeps me as his prisoner, I who'd race after him to hell; thinks I want to run away and betray him to everybody, can't believe in a motive that's not selfish, it's hard."

"You haven't, then, written to tell his father that you have found him?" I asked.

"God forgive me, no," he answered with a bent head; "though I have had chances to do it, too, mum, and the doctor must be in as much of a wonder what's come to me as what's come to Master Hanni. God forgive me! for never I'll forgive myself on this side Jordan. And all to pleasure the lad—but he can't see it, keeps me as a prisoner, it's hard."

"But what did he do in London? what did he think of the ladies there? was he really chased by the London people?" I asked, for I could not whisper my questions fast enough to satisfy my inquisitiveness.

Healy answered yes, that the sandals and bauge shirt of Shunter Island had been chased with hue and cry all up Tottenham Court Road at midday, and twice by night in other places; and that not the London police only were after him, for that he had no sooner stepped from the train down here than a constable laid hands on him; but he had filliped the constable in the face, and run away, making to the cave to get the "stele," which he seemed to be extremely eager to get, and then had run up here, dragging Healy with him.

"And he actually filliped the constable?" I said to Healy: "he is no longer, then, at all in awe of his 'Man'?"

I looked round at Hannibal Lepsius, and now saw his body all across the table, with one knee also on it, for, in the keenness of his strain as to that "stele," he had been pushing it inch by inch from him and following it; and now his brow was all brown and engorged, his eyes were glaring at the object like a maniac's, and now also a sort of groan broke out of his breast.

When I turned back to Healy to continue our conversation, I found that during those few moments that I had been looking away his brow had dropped in sleep; and I was just disengaging from his fingers the glass that he had been drinking from lest he should drop it, when I became aware of a tapping at the little door at the back. I stole out to it, I opened it, and now, heavens! my soul faints within me when I behold standing there the big Inspector Gibbon, together with that graceful young constable of Thring with the moustache, whose name is Shooter.

"We have found him at last," remarks Inspector Gibbon, for they had seen the light, climbed a little by the spout outside, and seen the young man poring over the stele.

"But what has he done?" I asked them, with a trembling about my right knee, hearing, as I asked it, Mrs. Bowden's clock strike twice.

"There are no less than five counts against him," answered Inspector Gibbon, "three from London, two down here; let's have the beauty out"—and he steps within the doorway.

At once now with a wild heart I darted back into Mrs. Bowden's room, to whisper to the young man, "I am afraid that two officers are come to arrest you!"

He groaned, without glancing up from his poring over that stone. I waited several seconds, hearing the clock tick, and my own heart as loudly pounding. Healy also, who had started awake, now sat staring with an open mouth.

"What shall I say to the two officers?" I asked the young man.

Again he groaned grievously, but did not glance up at me, and again I stood in suspense some seconds; till now he in an absent way, still without glancing up, mumbled at me, "Bring them here."

I ran out, and found the officers already at the door: in another moment they were standing within the housekeeper's room. Hanni Lepsius was now on his feet awaiting them, and the instant they appeared he stepped up to them, saying, "Now, I wish you to take me; take me—only be swift."

"Oh, come, no more of it," now said Inspector Gibbon, interrupting him with a good-natured disdain, drawing the young man away; and Hannibal Lepsius uttered no other word.

They were by this time not three feet from the old oak tree, Inspector Gibbon at the young man's right arm, Shooter at the left, keeping a strong grip, I could see, and a cautious guard, since they had been so warned; nor had I, for my part, the least expectation of seeing him escape them ere they reached the tree, or indeed at any time; but all at once, just as they reached the tree, without even the least effort I now beheld him easily free; and the next instant one saw a sight!—the two constables all entangled, and Hannibal Lepsius running furiously round and round the tree, ever with every revolution at a shorter distance from it, the rope in his hand, roping with many whorles the two men to the tree. I never was so curiously affected, I think, by any sight—with a feeling of religion and hallelujah, I may say, the two men's bulk of flesh looking so abject and helpless in the hands of that wit, like hippopotami with their insignificant skulls: though how he had contrived to escape out of their grasp without a struggle I still had no idea. To tie their hands, their arms being already bound, was to him not the work of a minute, and suddenly he was rushing back to the house, dashed inward past Healy and me without a word, and by the time we two had returned to Mrs. Bowden's room, he was already whining and whimpering anew over his stone, as if nothing had happened.

At this I felt myself fly red to the roots of my hair! for he meant the vial of vitriol which, procured at Wynton on the 27th, I have been foolishly fingering ever since.

"How should I know what is in the vial?" I said to Healy.

"Well, whatever it is," he said, "it is something that makes cloth rotten in a tick, for when you went out to tell the officers to come in, he dipped a match into the vial, drew with the match a circle on each of his shirt sleeves, and now, you see, the two pieces of shirt have disappeared"—and in truth the young man's arm nearest me was showing through a hole in his shirt, so I understood that by the working of the vitriol the two pieces of shirt had come away in the policemen's hands. I had begun to say, "Well, it was not so wonderful, after all, now that one knows how——" when one of the bound men began to shout out for succour; upon which Hanni Lepsius groaned within himself over his stone, and, without glancing up, told Healy to go and give them to know that if they made but one other outcry before the daybreak he would gag and agonise them; so Healy hastened out to say this, and thenceforth the two men remained mum.

At once, as I opened my eyes, he handed me the vial of vitriol, bowing a little, and smiling.

"What is this?" I asked him.

"It is oil of vitriol," replies the boy.

I ought, if I had had my wits, to have asked him why he handed it to me! but, being only half-awake and confused, I foolishly took the thing and put it down without finding a word to say; and I saw his gaze linger strangely upon me. Then he said, "I am very hungry."

I started! and I started anew when he said to me, "Hand this to that lady when she awakes."

"But what do you mean?" I said, shrinking from him; "do you, then, wish to outrage me? and do you suppose that I would do such a thing, really?"

"You will," he said; and to Healy, "Come."

"But stay!" I cried; "at what hour of the day do I see you?..."

36

He was already at the door of the room, but came back a little, saying, "At noon; and the marriage at two"—whereupon he anew picks up the vial of vitriol from the table, hands it to me, and goes through the door-way—the good God only knows why he did this.

I darted after, caught him at the back door, and, casting my arms about him, wet his cheek with my kisses and tears. He made no remark, save to say, "Do not release those police until twenty minutes past five"; and he went.

The moon had set, and the new day hardly yet dawning, but I could see him go past the oak tree without a glance at the two prisoners, and go away like ghosts, he and his Healy, through the swing-gate close by the south garden-wall.

It is now near seven, and here I still sit, even now not sleepy, for this is the day of my life. What is in my heart? Is it peace? Is it dancing? I think I have a fear....

It will soon be time to be at Miss Eve's bedside. Of course, I shall not give her the envelope, though he said with assurance that I will; but I have not as yet opened it to see what is in it, for I fear his consciousness of things.... There is something solid in it, like the half of a halfpenny, and a chain....

The 29th, at nine in the night. He has robbed me of my savings, he has abandoned me, he is gone for ever!... No, my God, I cannot write, my head cannot hold itself up.

The 30th. I will vitriolise him. God knows, that will not be easy, he has many eyes, it will be almost impossible: but those great men who make discoveries which amaze the creation—in what manner do they accomplish this? I think it is not because their wits are so vastly more than those of ordinary folk, but because their lives are wholly devoted to one thing only, as my life henceforth will be wholly devoted to this alone. God help me in this; it will be only after years of effort that I can even hope to do it, but one day, if God be my Helper, it will be done "al-right."

"Miss Vickery," I said, "can you tell me where my money is laid?"

Anew she lifts her eyes, looks at me silently, and from that look I knew at once that that phrase in the note had only been put into it so as to ensure that Miss Eve should receive the note; for he knew that I would open the envelope, and that Miss Eve knew nothing as to where my money is, for how could she? My money is in his pocket, that is where my money is, my two thousand francs.

The 31st. I was not allowed to get out of bed to-day, and ah, these English, they are frigid, they are hard on the surface, but beneath they are tenderer and better than all the world. I expected that Miss Ruth would lavish the compassion of her ever-wounded bosom upon my grief, but I have been even deeper touched by the goodness of Miss Eve. When, in one of the paroxysms, I cried, "Miss Vickery, I will vitriolise, I will vitriolise him, if it is in fifteen years to come!" she, with a look that flashed anger at me, began to say, "You shameful woman!" but then rushed to the bed and warmly embraced me in her arms, murmuring many times in words of wooing, "Poor bruised heart, poor wounded woman," with water swimming in her eyes, while I wept on her. A French lady would not have kissed me on the lips.... In the afternoon when I knew that she was below, I stole from bed, and, creeping to her boudoir, peeped in to see if the tissue-paper note with the half of a sovereign was yet on the card-table, whither she had brushed it from her; but it had vanished.

CHAPTER X.

The narrative of Jeanne Auvache, which continues yet through three volumes, may here be dropped, and what else took place may be gleaned from the "Memoirs" of Monsieur Goncourt Leflô (Prefect of the Seine), and from the "Notes" of Saïd Pasha (Chargé d'Affaires), together with jottings and gossips of other witnesses.

In that place which used, I think, to be called "La Plage," but is now the Club des Décavés, a crowd one afternoon sat surveying the Avenue du Bois de Boulogne. (The Décavés is far up at the top of the Avenue by the Arc de Triomphe, from which point the throngs of bicyclists who have toiled up the incline of the Champs Elysées put their legs up, give themselves to God, and by Him are taken gaily down the long-drawn-out incline to the Bois, like boats in the river of carriages which rolls droning down.) It was an afternoon in June, and everyone who knows his "capital of the universe" at all knows that sight, whose mood, in its large-minded worldliness, is rather to be recalled than to be described.

The Décavés itself, with people coming, going, sitting, sipping, gossiping, was a scene of no little vivacity; and to a new-comer, as he stepped up, one of a group of three said eagerly, "You have heard, Leflô?"

"But what an indiscretion!" cried Monsieur Isabeau Thiéry.

"A public embrace at the Foreign Office, my friends!" added the Abbé Sauriau, his plump palms spread a little.

"But, then, everything is possible at the Foreign Office," remarked the Prefect of the Seine: "above all, dizziness of the head."

"This, however, my friends," now said the old Duc de Rey-Drouilhet, "is an incident, not of the Third Republic, but of the Second Empire! Transfer the scene to the Bal Morel, and the lady might have been Païva, as the male Plon-Plon," whereat Isabeau Thiéry shook backward his lion's mane of hair with, "It may be an incident of the Third Empire, which we see beginning—unless by chance a patriot or two still exists in France." ("He was"—to quote from the "Notes" of Saïd Pasha—"one of the tribe of poet-politicians—the Hugos, Lamartines, Châteaubriands—and though neither his poetry, nor even his politics, was at all equal to theirs, Thiéry, as we know, took himself awfully seriously, excelling them all, since not in head, at any rate in hair, in his spread of hatrim and La Vallière cravat, whose crimson hue proved him "of the Left.")

"A propos of 'the clock,'" remarked the old Duc de Rey-Drouilhet, his little hand all aflash with diamonds in the sunshine, "Freycinet *fils* is said to have remarked this afternoon at Tortoni's that then at least, during the kiss, Monsieur Lepsius lost reckoning of the clock, seeing that his eyes were tight closed! And it is now being said round about the Palais-Bourbon of Cardinal Pontmartin, who has declared that the kiss lasted a minute and eight seconds by the clock, 'How could the Prelate have seen the clock, when those holy eyes of his must have been poring upon Paradise revealed before them!'—a *mot* at which the titter and grin of the beau set his (!) teeth atremble with a rather ghastly glitter on his gums.

"But, Monsieur le Duc, they were not polished by myself," replied Saïd Pasha innocently—a reply which raised a smile! since everybody knew that the duke, in the course of a very varied career, had had need to be his own menial.

"In any case, you can enlighten us as to the identity of the lady who is on the tapis in connection with a certain individual," said Isabeau Thiéry to Saïd Pasha, who at that time was generally supposed to be in quite the inner *côterie* of the Palais-Lepsius; but in the same instant that the staid and cautious *chargé d'affaires* was asking what lady was meant, the duc was saying, "Here, too, comes Monsieur the Englishman," and one Mr. E. Reader Meade, an attaché at the Faubourg St. Honoré, walked up—a man who, because of his bulk, and of that mass of face on which was written "phlegm" and "judgment," was often in the Paris of that day nicknamed "the Englishman." As he approached, the aged gossip, holding up his eye-glass before a dilapidated eye, made the observation, "But do I read aright in Monsieur Meade's air that he is unaware of anything having happened?"

"Such a kiss," the Abbé Sauriau said, "is a proof, my friends, of nothing save of Lepsius' disdain of mankind, since he certainly weighed the thirty or so pairs of eyes which observed that kiss as lightly as lovers on a stile weigh the eyes of kine which watch them. Do you know the story that is told of his answer to Marshal Macintosh, à propos of the Marshal's remark that a foreigner, even after a hundred years, is never regarded and behugged by the French as a Frenchman? Lepsius replied, 'It may be nice

40

to be loved, monsieur, but what is nicer far is to be disliked, to behold yourself surrounded by people thirsting like Tantalus to hurt you, and to behold them powerless, because of your towering superiority.' So you see, my friends: Napoleon regarded men mainly as pawns in his game; Monsieur Lepsius, in his more *savant* mood, regards them as gorillas in his garden of zoology"—and now the abbé's eyes shot out beneath his bush of eyebrow a beam of bile, bush that burned, yet was not consumed, while Isabeau Thiéry's eyes, quick as tinder, caught fire also, for company.

At this Monsieur Leflô—a little quick personality, whose hairs grew like a wig of bristles—ogled Isabeau Thiéry with, "We are all aware that the utiliser of the moon has a champion wherever Saïd Pasha is present!"

"But, Monsieur le Prefect," said Saïd Pasha, sudden and quick in quarrel, "am I charged with partisanship for aught but the simple truth?"

"No, monsieur," replied the Prefect dryly, "even though it is a matter of common talk that Saïd Pasha once shed tears of admiration at the sight of a certain individual racing with camels from a sand-storm near Khartoum, and from that moment became a hero-worshipper. So it is said—I was not there. In any case, I beg leave to question the 'magnetic gale' by which you explain this embrace, since I believe that the reason of it is quite a different one than people conceive."

"Oh, as for that," Leflô answered in his off-hand way, "it requires no spy of the Rue de Jerusalem to recognise the truth that this kiss was no result of vertigo, but of a political purpose."

"That is only the truth," added the old Due de Rey-Drouilhet, "since it is certain that a certain individual 'knows his Paris'—more perfectly knows it than Napoleon the First, as perfectly perhaps as Napoleon the Third; and knowing that your Parisian, as Victor Hugo has observed, must for ever be grinning the teeth, either in a laugh or in a snarl, the arch-gamester never permits himself to forget that there must be no flagging in the game, since in Paris to be out of sight is to be out of mind, and so seeks continually to *épater les gens*, keeping himself alive in the public eye by breaking ever anew upon it in a new attitude and costume, and invariably with an *éclat* whose radiance blinds. No, this gentleman is hardly one of those who like to shine in the dark! If for once in his life he tears his lips from the telephone to apply them to those of a lady, he takes care that there shall be as many eye-witnesses to the event as when some months ago he used to assume the rôle of Haroun al Raschid by appearing in an incognito of rags in the thieves' kitchens of the Quartier Mouffetard, where he engaged in a knife-fight with a Spaniard, and in a cangiar-fight with two Moors who had attacked him. For here, my friends, we meet with the scenic skill of a Bonaparte in combination with the ambitious mania of a Thiers, Bismarck's steel, that art-genius for *Welt-politik* of a Cæsar Borgia, and——"

"Yes, last August," said Mr. E. Reader Meade, gazing away at all the throng and flutter of the scene, "last August, when the individual in question had not yet been two months a factor in politics; but nine biggish months of world-knowledge, of archive-searching, of worming in the Big Book,[B] have since gone by——"

To words so bold no one answered anything, till Isabeau Thiéry observed, "From the bee honey, though, as aroma from the rose, though the former *has* its sting, as the latter its thorn."

"Ah, monsieur," answered the Abbé Sauriau, knowing on which nerve to work upon Thiéry, "Brutuses, I fear, are even rarer than Cæsars!" whereat, instantly, Isabeau Thiéry, with a new enthusiasm, was crying, "Still, Monsieur l'Abbé, Brutuses—exist!"

But now, before the anecdotist could further go, a sound arose and grew, not loud, but universal over the grounds of the Club, the Avenue, l'Etoile—a rumour in whose droning the word "Lepsius" was to be heard, as a troop of Zouaves and Turcos, riding all in their bright robes, broke into the ocean-current of carriages that rolled through the Avenue. Up from the Elysées they came, making down for the Bois de Boulogne; and up soon after them trotted another crowd of troopers—Moors, Hindoos—voluminous in their vestments of various hues, carrying javelins (jereeds), with streamers, on large chargers which caracoled; and, close behind these, three carriages with gentlemen-ushers, household gentlemen; and up behind these outriders; grooms costumed in green and gold; pigmies in jockey-caps, from which hung fringes of gold; and up behind all a phaeton hauled by Orloff horses that haughtily pawed the air, to fling far their front-hoofs, trotting. In this sat Lepsius. He was in mufti, but clearly no "mere *pékin*," the insignia of the Grand Cordon of the Legion showing his connection with the Army; and by his side sat a girl who looked American, on her lap a scribbling-book, and flying in her fingers

42

a pencil. He, as he drove up, bowed repeatedly a little to the buzz that droned about his ear, but without ever once glancing upward, his lips never ceasing to move and murmur to the girl whose fingers flew. And away to the wood swept the wind of it.

"'Lepsius'?" Isabeau Thiéry breathed the word.

"*Need* I explain," said Monsieur le Comte, taking a chair, all business, all smiles, with dimples in the chart of his large face, "that there may be many men of that name?—*not* necessarily related by ties of family? which ties, in any case, can never possess much weight in the matter of politics. So that if by chance we here are all a harmony, politically speaking——"

The count's eye ran prying with an underlook about the table from face to face, whereat Mr. E. Reader Meade glanced at Saïd Pasha, Saïd Pasha glanced at Mr. Meade, and they two got up to bow themselves out of the business, while the others, with glances at one another, silently smiled.

"Gentlemen," suddenly rising, said Dr. Lepsius in a low tone, "I think that perhaps if I took a stroll while you talk the matter over, that might be more in order. I will be back to answer any question that may occur to you," whereat hats were anew raised, the doctor went away, Monsieur de Courcy's underlook peered about to see that nobody was too near, and now he drew with care from out a pocket-book a bit of paper, rather brown and brittle, that had passed through flame. He laid it on the table: and quickly, like a congress of eagles, the intriguers' heads were together over it, the old duke skipping like a youth closer round to it, and that lax skin of the Abbé Sauriau's brow, which above was narrow, broad below, twitching short-sightedly over the browned words, while his bush burned. Only the Count de Courcy leaned back, fingering his secret crucifix, musing through his cigarette fumes upon the clouds, humorously dimpled. ("He was ever healthy and happy-hearted when in office-harness," says Saïd Pasha of him, "with a no small degree of rush and magnetism when revelling in the thick of affairs; one of your true *gens de bureau*; an intellect essentially narrow, bigot, bourgeois, as 'devout' as he was profoundly irreligious; but iron; and the busier the blither.")

"But can we be sure who wrote it?" Isabeau Thiéry said, "when it lacks a signature?" to which the count stopped his humming to reply, "Would a signature add to our certainty, monsieur, when the individual whom you have in your mind is said to write a hundred hands a day, as it suits his purpose? But surely the internal evidence furnishes us with a certainty which is ample."

"Oh, ample," said Monsieur Leflô, glancing up.

"Well, he is a showman," sighed the old gossip, rising with satisfied old eyes from the script, while his eye-glass dropped.

"But he is mad," added the Abbé Sauriau.

"Well, it is a great and a gallant brain, after all," cried Isabeau Thiéry with a flush, when Monsieur le Comte had put away his pocket-book with the script in it.

"A great and a gallant brain," mused the Minister of the Interior, who, fingering his imperial, was smiling at the sky; "though not a Christian, not a Catholic, not a French brain."

"Tush! the brain of a precocious, pert youth," observed the Abbé Sauriau, with a burning bush, "whom it is the duty of us all to remove out of harm's way without more delay."

"Though that will not be done without difficulty, mind you!" Monsieur Leflô remarked with a little grimace, planting his fore finger-tip against his hard nut: "but in the event of a citation of the individual before the Sixth Correctional Tribunal, with a view to obtaining a decree of banishment against him for instigating civil strife, I should say that this document would be of use."

"The Sixth Correctional Tribunal," mused the count, smiling; "I thought, however, that that idea had by this time been abandoned by us all, if only for the reason that the trial could not possibly be completed before the Exhibition, during which, as we assume, the *coup d'état* that we dread is to take place? Personally I cannot help thinking that a court-trial of uncertain termination is no longer pertinent to the situation, especially as we have been so happy as to win the sanction of the Church (in the persons of Monsieur l'Abbé and of Monseigneur) to move urgent and more certain ways of averting this danger to the world."

The Abbé Sauriau, who had a habit of ever eyeing his right shoe and red sock, which shook up continually (the leg being crossed), struck smartly with his gloves, remarking, "A stronghold close to the coast, with grim bastions and the gloomiest of oubliettes! twelve or fifteen years of that is what the youth wants——" and he struck back his spread of hair that broadened lankly out down over the ears, the Count de Courcy repeating with approval in his musing manner, "Twelve to fifteen years of that, twelve to fifteen years——" and going suddenly grim-red, he giggled gleefully to himself.

"Monsieur l'Abbé is right," the old Duc de Rey-Drouilhet said: "fifteen years of a bastille's oubliette is known to induce in a youth a definite diffidence as to using his lips in public, either in speaking or in kissing," at which speech Monsieur de Courcy, who was drinking menthe, grew crimson, gripping his glass so grimly that it cracked, the green fluid streaming from the table to the abbé's sock.

"If it can be done ..." muttered Monsieur Leflô; "*if* it can be done...."

"Why, Monsieur le Prefect," said the abbé, "was it not a Frenchman who said that 'cannot' is a *bête de mot*?"

"That is a truth, too, monsieur!" cried Isabeau Thiéry, "and provided it prove necessary...."

"The young Lepsius?"

"Yes, Monsieur l'Abbé—your hero."

"Whose hero?"

"Is it not being stated on the boulevards by Léon Bergerac in particular, who is always the best informed man in Paris, that you are bitten by an infatuation which is half an idolatry of admiration, and half a hatred, and wholly a hankering, that hardly permits you to talk of aught but of one being?"

"*I?*" breathed the Abbé Sauriau, standing still to stare, revealed a moment to himself; then with rage, "oh, he lies, he lies: Léon Bergerac is known to be my enemy!"

"Well, well, no doubt," muttered the minister "... but as to this woman, whose name is Auvache——"

"Not the Jeanne Auvache who threw vitriol at the individual in question at Dover on the 11th of November, threw it wide, and was imprisoned for five months?" queried Monsieur l'Abbé.

The Abbé Sauriau pondered it for some moments, and presently observed, "She must be an imbecile."

"That is what I have said to myself, Monsieur l'Abbé," replied the minister; "why else should the woman, in wishing to obtain an *entrée* into the *valetaille* Lepsius, address herself to *me*? unless by some chance she is

45

aware that I know one Nundcumar, a functionary in the Palais-Lepsius....
This Nundcumar has risen, Monsieur l'Abbé. Eight years ago he was a
lean scarecrow down on his luck about Paris and London, pretending to
be a doctor of medicine, but possessing even less knowledge of medicine
than the present Prefect of Police possesses of the police. Then he became a cook, and it was thus that I again came across him at Egmond,
the Brittany château of the Comtesse de Pichegru-Picard. Then he remi-
grated to his native Agra, and was there met and admired by the individual whom we now have in our minds—so Nundcumar avers, though this
person, who never ceases to speak, certainly never yet produced a word
which by chance was an accuracy. At all events, I am still in touch with
the man, and could easily induce him—to-day even—to introduce that ill-
used and lunatic woman into the *valetaille* Lepsius, provided I do not def-
initely find in my interview with her presently that she has any purpose in
view other than the search for work."

"You have known how to say what I was only able to think, Monsieur
l'Abbé.... Au revoir, then." And the Count de Courcy drove away.

The abbé then turned to go back to the table of the gossips; but now
a little girl who was gambolling among the trees, tumbling down before
his feet and beginning to scream, immediately he had her garnered in his
arms, hugging her to his bosom, his lips on her head, with whimperings
of love ("for," says a Note of Saïd Pasha, "he had a most fond father's
heart, if especially for children, hardly less for all the world, whenever
he was not merciless with envy of some other mind"); and he toyed before the child's eyes one of his few coins, saying, "But look, then, all this
is for thee—all, all," and he pointed at the receding brougham, leering,
breathing, "Look! that is the brougham of Monsieur the Minister of the
Interior—but look! a man whose 'blood boils to speak of these turpitudes'
since he has need to condone his deeds to his own shabby-genteel con-
science"—and he clasped the little girl's fingers upon the franc, placed her
on the ground, and now hurried back to the table where by now Dr. Lepsius was again sitting with the gossips.

CHAPTER XI.

THE CHAMBER-WINDOW.

At that very time Shan Healy was speeding on a bicycle (having missed a train) from Paris to Versailles, with perspiration raining over his face and swear-words vented when racing through those villages paved with old pavers, which mercilessly jerked him. It was not until six o'clock that he got to Versailles and the Villa des Medicis there, a house of the Comtesse de Pichegru-Picard, where, having scorched down to the house-front through a great avenue of yews, he craved to interview Miss Ruth Vickery.

He was taken to the door of a chamber in the middle of which stood three ladies talking warmly, though in low tones—two elderly ladies and Miss Ruth Vickery; and a whirl of words was being uttered among them, sometimes all the three trying to make their opinions heard at once, all looking as exhausted and haggard as if they had been going on all the day long, while in the gloom of a far corner of the room lay Miss Eve Vickery asleep, with an appearance of exhaustion, even of swoon. Shan Healy stood on the threshold, and he could just hear the Comtesse de Pichegru-Picard, whom he knew very well, cry with a casting up of her hands and eyes, "Ah, my dear Lina, you can persuade an angel or the good God himself to change their mind, but you cannot persuade a saint who is English too."

"But, Aunt," wooed Miss Ruth, "bear with me, since I do mean well, as in my God's sight. Ask yourself—how can I, how could I, try to induce Eve to marry a man who, it appears, is without even morality, whose mood is pagan, whose aim is Cæsarian, whose God is arrogance?... And Eve never would, I think, if I know her! You have heard her say yourself——"

"Ah, then, why in the good God's name did the girl go and kiss him with all Paris gazing at it?" exclaimed the Comtesse de Pichegru-Picard.

"Aunt," breathed Miss Ruth, all ruby-red, with drooped lids, "you know that Eve did not—'kiss'— him; he—'kissed'—her."

"Ah, my good Ruth," observed the third lady, one Madame Lina Grammont, "the world does not draw these exquisite distinctions, believe

47

me: it knows that in a kiss it is generally the gentleman who both begins against the lady's will and ends against her will."

"Exactly," remarked the Comtesse de Pichegru-Picard; "but then, we all know our English: it is always their little mannerism to regard the lady as made of anything but of flesh and blood. The fact, however, that stares one in the face is that Eve is now bound to be married immediately; and I repeat that the scandal will be less if of the two gentlemen she chooses the one who has kissed her."

"So I hear you say, my dear," replied the countess, "though Eve herself no doubt most accurately knows her own secret; but if it be a fact that her stomach is such as to like the Comte de Courcy better, why will she not send for him, since he is every hour expecting her reply?"

"She will send, I think," replied Miss Ruth. "What, however, was the use of summoning papa from London unless she is to hold out for his presence before pronouncing her decision? He should by now have arrived in Paris, and within an hour will be in Versailles; then, I think, she will speak, she will send, for she feels, I am sure, the nobleness of Monsieur de Courcy's renewed offer, and will not, I think, grieve him by any longer——"

"You do not believe, Healy, I see, that such a union could be good?" said Miss Ruth, her gaze on his face.

"Well, to be frank, no, miss, marriage wouldn't hardly suit him," said the voluble Healy. "No, no; he'd be that miserable, you wouldn't believe; and the fonder he was of the lady, the more he'd hate and hiss at her for making him waste time. Time's his wife; the clock, the clock, miss. Believe me, only to be near him, people feel in a prickly heat themselves, as if they were breathing fever from some fierce atmosphere—the very Orientals in the palace, miss, only that slothful old story-teller, Nundcumar.... No, no, miss, do now, he'll be that miserable——"

"And his lady, too, I think, Healy?" suggested Miss Ruth, with her smile.

At this Miss Vickery, with her stare of child-wonder, stared at Healy, muttering, "How very much lighter and kinder would he feel, now, if he had no keys, nor any jewels to lay up for himself!"

"Doubtless, miss," said the other; "but that's how it stands—what would you have? What was I saying? Oh, about that night in the forest round about the ruined town of Anuradhapura; yes, that's a forest, miss, if you like—boundless; but I think I've told you about that night before, miss, often; and from that night he has been good friends with me, till two days ago, when the doctor came——"

"Does he still avoid a meeting with his father?" asked Miss Vickery in a voice of secrecy.

"Steal softly in," breathed Miss Ruth to Healy; and softly she herself, having moved into the room, stole on tip-toe quite to the telephone, the opening of which she shut off and stuffed up, Miss Eve meanwhile seeming still asleep; and to Healy Miss Ruth now said aloud, "Continue now, Healy, to speak of your master's treatment of his poor father."

Healy looked at her, and, discerning her meaning, whispered to himself, "Why, if she isn't as wise as a serpent!"

Miss Vickery, with her face averted from the narrator, held her eyes bent skyward with a steadfast gaze, begging for God's forgiveness of men; but from Miss Eve, who must have heard, who was meant to hear, neither word was uttered, nor a stir seen.

Now, however, that stream of Healy's speech was checked by the appearance in the doorway of a gentleman neatly dressed in grey, with a grey top-hat on his head, a neat umbrella, and side-whiskers, with him being the Comtesse de Pichegru-Picard and Madame Grammont; and Healy, seeing him, murmured, "Your pa, miss," and now bowed himself out; while Mr. Vickery, darting his eyes all about the room, and discerning in the gloom his younger girl on the couch, rushed by Miss Ruth without any greeting, his eyes brimming with tears, his mouth trembling, and on his knees garnering Miss Eve in his arms, gave way now to weeping, again and again darting down his lips at her mouth, with pausings to gaze at her face, then again darting down at her mouth, with mania.

Miss Eve sat up, breathing "papa," and laughed a little, casting back some hairs from her brow with a gesture which, undoubtedly, was not without something of hectic and hare-brained. Indeed, she appeared that day to be dwelling in a region so infected with fever, that through the day she had been treated as a patient, and on the sick list.

"Well, here I am," Mr. Vickery said to her, "just arrived by God's help—in time, I hope.... Got a headache, have you? my soul? my love?"

Miss Eve smiled triumphantly in her parent's face, replying, "No, papa; why should I?"

"Did you, papa?" asked Miss Eve, smiling with her father.

"Yes. Eve, have I done well?"

"Why, papa, I think so," replied Miss Eve, smiling that defiance which is amused, that triumph which is secure. "Monsieur de Courcy is a most estimable man."

"He is; but still, Eve, tell me, tell me, dear—have I done well?"

"Oh, I quite think so, papa.... Have you had a pleasant trip across?"

"No, no, let us be frank now; let us make use of plain terms, let's not mince matters, Eve; come now, tell your papa—my own, my sweet—will you have de Courcy?"

"Oh, as to that, why, I think so, papa," replied Miss Eve with some appearance of surprise about the eye-brows. "I thought that that was rather understood as a settled thing: ask Ruth, ask aunt: they'll tell you that Monsieur de Courcy, that model of morals, high at the head of my list, hasn't a rival to dread."

Upon this the father turned with an opening of the arms toward the other ladies, saying, "Why, this is well.... You didn't tell me!"

No reply was made to him; only the Comtesse de Pichegru-Picard exchanged half a smile with Madame Grammont, who just shrugged, while Miss Ruth remained with her eyelids drooped.

The young lady, contemplating her father's face with a calm smile, replied, "Quite settled, papa—for *my* share. If it *can* be, it shall be."

"'*Can* be?' What does she mean?"—Mr. Vickery threw this whisper at the other ladies behind him; but before anything further could be uttered, a bomb was hurled into the *salon* by the words of a servant who entered, saying "Monsieur Lepsius to talk with Mr. Vickery"—and he handed a card.

Straight sprang Mr. Vickery up, Miss Eve also raising herself by degrees, and all with blanched cheeks gaped in silence at the menial, till Mr. Vickery, his visage rushing into crimson, cried in a high and hysteric kind of cry, "Say to that gentleman that Mr. Vickery, being engaged, begs him to state his business by letter!"

The menial bowed and backed out, and immediately now there reigned a gale of breaths among the ladies, Madame Grammont and the countess making a thousand gesticulations together, Mr. Vickery standing again pale-faced by a reaction, Miss Ruth at him instigating him to be grim, Miss Eve moving about from place to place, reading the titles of books, glancing at trees outside, glancing at looking-glasses.

It lasted four minutes, which seemed much more, after which the menial was once more there, bearing a note scribbled in pencil, whose folds Mr. Vickery tremblingly opened. Miss Ruth meantime breathing in his ear, "Pray, papa, do not read it aloud!"—words which Miss Eve either heard or surmised, for now immediately she muttered with some huff, "Oh, I have no wish to hear anything," and went away.

It was Madame Grammont who, gifted with the strongest eyesight, read the note aloud in a monotone, the gloaming in the room having now grown very heavy; and as she finished, and all raised their eyes, all started, for there afresh was Miss Eve, who had been seen to leave the chamber, hovering anew near to hear.

"I am not to be browbeaten!" suddenly cried Mr. Vickery in a high kind of cry.

"Ah, papa, no agitation, papa!" Miss Ruth called through a throat whose music broke.

"I say I am not to be browbeaten, I am not to be threatened!" screamed Mr. Vickery querulously afresh in an ecstasy, for the atmosphere was all electric, and each one present caught from all the rest a hectic cheek and a lip of quivering.

"My God, I foresaw all! and my advice was not followed," cried the Comtesse de Pichegru-Picard, with a casting up of the hands.

"'The files of life,' 'the drift of fate'!" Madame Grammont muttered in a maze.

"Calm, papa, calm!" called out Miss Ruth anew: "ah, how disastrous! papa, I warn you, this agitation is fatal to the welfare of the soul!"

"Oh, Ruth, let one alone!" now said the countess in an irritation without restraint; "it is you who are the cause of all, at the end of the tale."

"Aunt, I?" asked Miss Ruth, with reproach lodged in the soul of her eyes.

"But no, Margaret, but no," protested Madame Grammont: "it is not the fault of Ruth, it is not the fault of Ruth."

"Let me get my girl out of this infernal country!" now cried out the high-strung Mr. Vickery; "it is France that has done this!"

"Oh, but be reasonable, Matthieu, at the end of the tale!" the countess mouthed, with intolerance.

"Quite right, papa," now cried out Miss Eve in a spirit of rollicking and recklessness, "let us clearly prove to everyone that we act in no 'humour of freak,' having a will of our own!"

"My love!" cried Mr. Vickery.

"'The files of life,'" mused Madame Grammont anew; "'humour of freakishness'!"

"Ah, but he is right, believe me!" cried the Comtesse de Pichegru-Picard; "he has his meaning! he knows Eve better than she knows herself."

"You and others may *think* so, Aunt," called Miss Eve, snapping her thumb and finger daintily up in the air, with a wheel on her feet.

"But he may still be there!" said Madame Grammont; "is he still there at the door, Gabriel?"

"Monsieur Lepsius has departed, madame," the gaudy Gabriel gave answer, who through all this had stood there with a bowed brow.

"What happened in the hall?" asked the countess. "Did Monsieur Lepsius make any attempt to enter?"

"Monsieur Lepsius desired to enter, madame," answered Gabriel, "when I gave him Mr. Vickery's reply that it might be better for him to state his business by letter; but on his attempt to force an entrance, both Baptiste and myself barred his advance with our arms outspread, and he then, after staring a moment into our faces, broke into a laugh, hastily wrote the note that has been handed you, and drove very quickly away."

"Did Monsieur Lepsius utter any remark at all?" Madame Grammont began to ask, but before the words were well uttered, there had entered another flunky, who came to proclaim the presence of Monsieur de Courcy at the door; whereupon—a renewed flutter and flurry of consultation! until the ladies rushed from the room, leaving Mr. Vickery to receive the visitor; and immediately in came the Minister of the Interior with his brisk and breezy air, but about his brow now a shade of deliberation.

They two then conversed together until the hour when the dinner-gong began to sing out, whereupon the ladies in their bravery came sailing in, smirking as superbly now as personalities translated beyond the concerns of earth; and after a little small-talk the visitor stepped away with them to dinner.

However, they had not well moved out of the room when now the telephone-rattle in the alcove started to prattle, upon which Mr. Vickery with passion in his heart darted back to it, and Miss Eve also doubled back to be near, though remaining far from her father in the centre of the apartment, staring.

"Who are you?" called Mr. Vickery, the receiver at his ear.

The answer was "Lepsius," and even Miss Eve, though hovering away off in the middle of the room, could hear it in thunder, for the speaker now no doubt lay in his whispering-gallery, where the sound-waves from his mouth, focusing themselves upon his telephone, struck monstrous rough, their grumble trumpeting unease upon Mr. Vickery's ear-drum with the gutturalness of some grum god thundering; and, "I want to speak with Miss Eve Vickery," grumbled the thunder.

"It is Mr. Vickery who hears you!"

"I know; allow one to speak with Miss Eve, Mr. Vickery!"

Now with wide eyes hied Miss Eve on tip-toe nigh, hissing, "*Say I am at dinner, papa!*"

"Miss Eve Vickery is about to sit down to dinner," Mr. Vickery cried, with stricter accuracy.

"She will not eat much!... But as for you, Mr. Vickery, will you have me for a son-in-law?"

"The proposal sounds abrupt, Monsieur Lepsius!"

"Why so? How much waste of time is necessary? And what is your complaint against me? I quite fail to gather this."

"It cannot be discussed over the telephone!"

"Why can it not? Is it that you are offended with me for kissing your daughter?"

"*S-s-s-s-s, sir!*... But I am being awaited at dinner, Monsieur Lepsius!"

"It was not I who wished to kiss her, it was she who wished to kiss me!"

"Eve, go! go!" screamed Mr. Vickery, warding his daughter away with one arm.

"Say, papa," Miss Eve hissed, reaching far forward to her father's ear with her cheeks afire, "that I am affianced to a good and gallant gentleman!"

"My daughter——" Mr. Vickery commenced to call.

"Tell Miss Eve, sir," the thunderer rumbled, "that I can hear each word that she utters, and that I know she does not mean one syllable of any one of them."

"I have to wish you good evening, Monsieur Lepsius!" cried Mr. Vickery with a high-pitched cry.

"Go, if you choose; but you prove yourself a feeble and foolish old pantaloon, you know."

"And you, sir, a courteous young gentleman!" upon which Mr. Vickery put up the receiver, and went with one cheek-bone branded rosy, and one blanched, Miss Eve smiling, with her eyes alight, by his side.

The meal was then eaten serenely by all, after which, in the midst of Parisian chat in the salon, it was found not impossible to bring about, without intention, a *tête-à-tête* between Miss Eve and the Minister of the Interior; and Monsieur de Courcy, having come through this with success, remained still on, the merriest of ministers and men, until close on eleven o'clock, when, hunted down by a mounted officer with a cipher, he made his bows, and went away.

"Who is it?" she hoarsely hissed, for outside the shutter a tap had sounded.

"I! Open!" some chest panted to her, and she knew him, yet anew she hissed with all her wild heart in her windpipe, *"Who is it? What is it?"*

"The staple to which I hang is giving to my weight," the chest gasped: "forty seconds and I fall a corpse."

In ten Lepsius had leapt within the window....

He, looking up to the window, threw out to her the whisper, "You are wise! You are witty!" upon which she sprang up to throw out to him the whisper, "Do not come across the bed!" for he stood now with one knee on it, and she could see him in a ray of the moon as she had first beheld him at The Towers in a red shirt loose about the neck and belt, without any jacket or hat; and he, too, could see her in shadow at the window.

"Did I not help you to escape?" he asked her; and then disjointedly, "Do you wear the half-coin which I sent you?"

Miss Eve gave no reply, getting by degrees her breath again in silence.

"Did you know in your heart," he asked her, "that I would come to-night? You were waiting up for me, playing the fiddle; it was that Andante of Mendelssohn; you played it four times over."

54

"Lepsius, you must go," Miss Eve said.

"I will go near the peep of day, and you with me!"

"No, now; and without me, I think."

"Oh, you are cold," he replied, "and I hate your stone's heart: cold by nature, and colder by hypocrisy that penetrates your texture to the core of you. Oh, I know and foreknow you to my agony, negative, null, enigmatic, like a watch which won't go, though one goads it, and finally one crushes it under a rock; as frigid as that water of a mortal quality which drips from a rock in the territory of Nonacris; or like that bag——"

"I did not think," Miss Eve rejoined, leaning both her elbows on the window's sill, "that you were such a silly boy."

He during some seconds did not answer this, drew back a bit from the bed with a bent head, reflecting, and then said, "Well, it is silly, it is self-sacrifice; and yet—curious! while I fought against you, since it is silly, I thought it sillier than after I gave in to you. Silly, indeed, I still see it, for these feelings of love make the blood to flow from the front of the brain to other caves of the frame—ruinously! so that loving is a reverting to lower-animal natures whose brains are less largely furnished with blood, the sense of romance and poetry in loving being due to some umbra of remembrance in us of old brutes, moons, and moods, of the geologic ooze, the deluge, the roll in the Jurassic morass, the rufous Vesuvius, the gloomy lagoon, when the moon glowed more big and close to this globe. Love is thus a fall and relapse; and yet—curiously——"

Miss Eve, her face half concealed with her palm, asked, "But *what* is fated? that is the question. We imagine that what we wish is fated."

Here Miss Eve smiled, remarking dryly, "Lepsius, you are full of apes."

"Aren't you? Isn't the world?" he asked; upon which she said, "Yes, I know your low view of men—and of women, I suppose, still more; but beside my *élancé* upper-shape, my thigh-bone, my chin, my faded old air and hoary disdain of iris, I have a mind, which is jealous of your omission to mention it."

"I meant to mention it!"

"Oh?" says she, "that was too sweet of you. Last but not least?"

"By no means least!" he answered earnestly: "a mind, I am certain, better than mine."

"Ah, now you are insincere," she said.

"Mine un——! But what, then, is 'education' in your view?" she wished to know.

"Education," he told her, "is a waking of one's subconsciousness to consciousness. I, for instance, know nothing that you do not—or not much; but I am much more conscious of what we both know. Tell me, now—whereabouts were you twenty-four hours since?"

"But you remember——" Miss Eve started to say, but now, startled by some sound, breathed eagerly to him, "*did you hear something?*"

"It is a mouse going down the right sound-hole of your violin," he replied; and now Miss Eve anew leaned her elbow on her window-sill to continue saying, "But you remember that all this you started to utter of *me*, then continued with 'they,' 'they'; since then, as 'they' are so *I*, why are you there by my bed?"

"But are you not in all things far above me?" he asked, "save in this of a wakeful consciousness?"

"But this of a wakeful consciousness," said she, "is everything, is it not? It is this which makes the difference between a genius and an ape, a god and a dog, you believe, do you not? And you have it, and not I. Only a thigh-bone I own, let me be thrown to a dog."

"What Man is that?" Miss Eve asked, frowning, her wits rather winded now and flustered at the speed of her speaker's thoughts.

"Do you love me?" Miss Eve asked him in a whisper, leaning now far out of her window to him, who leaned near to her.

"Beloved," Lepsius groaned, and again, "beloved.... When I came home from the Quai d'Orsay last night, I dropped down in a drowse, and, with the feast of your kiss still warm in my mouth, I thought in my dream that your feet walked with mine athwart fields of asphodel in future far, far off under a forlorn and morphia moon—I could not tell you. Then in the dark of the morning I awaked, and you were not there in my arms. I passed my palm thrice across my bed of straws, but you were nowhere there; so I had the thought that my darling might be in the garden, among the lilies by the lake, gazing up at my casement, a thought half-crazy, half-drowsy; but up I bounded and raced all round the palace-walls, gazing down into the gardens in order to spy you out and call you up, and you were nowhere there. If one of the spokes of the kite-contrivance on which

I fly had not been broken, I should have flown to you. But I ran down, got out, and began to run to you; and the *sergents de ville* must have asked themselves where Lepsius was rushing to under the morning stars, with half a thought, perhaps, in their heart's heart of a *coup d'état*."

"You didn't come," Miss Eve observed.

"No," he answered, "I turned back; four leagues to Versailles, and I had already lost a good deal of time on your account.... Eve, I have lost hours."

"Bomb of *poudre Rachel*," Lepsius mumbled with a chuckle; "so you came to an arrangement with de Courcy this evening?"

"Yes, then," Miss Eve said, *her* left shoulder, too, shaken a second by a chuckle.

"And the same night you admit another lover to your bed-chamber!" he said, chuckling.

"Oh, well," she muttered with lowered lids, chuckling within one shoulder, and they chuckled one with the other.

"Are ladies, then, restrained by no scruples as to justice?" Lepsius asked. "Delighter in lies! enigma! through what abstruse movement of your bosom did you get yourself into this embroglio? Not that it matters; but you will inflict a sense of injury upon this man, who has done you no injury," a speech at which in one instant Miss Eve flew into a passion, and, leaning forth, thrice struck the window-sill imperiously, crying through a gruff throat, "As God is my witness——"

"Sh-h-h," Lepsius went.

"Let me speak!" she imperiously hissed: "I mean to marry him, do you hear it? Heaven be my witness!" and up she threw her eyes, trembling as she held them bent on high.

"Eve, no," said Lepsius gently: "you do not mean to do that; you believe that you do, but meantime in your subconsciousness you firmly confide in me never to permit such an absurdity, and so can afford to boast and be wayward.... Dear, would it not certainly kill us both?"

"If it kills a host I will do it!" Miss Eve heatedly replied; "never through life have I broken a promise, nor now shall begin with a vow; given and pledged is my troth; God be my witness in this."

"But *why* did you give it and pledge it? I can't guess!"

"Because I chose!"

"Cogent waste of three words!"

"I shall never have *you*, anyway!" she said with a nod and threat of the head.

"And why?" he asked in a bewilderment.

"Because you despise my mind!" she sharply replied.

"I have already explained why that is quite impossible," he made answer.

"Oh, woman knows her own secret, and people's explanations make no impression upon her intuitions. You despise my mind; and there's this still deeper reason against any getting together of you and me, that I despise yours."

"I despise it, too; yet I endure it."

"Oh!" she sighed, "that untrue humility of yours, it irritates me to the soul, till I hate! ... doubly untrue because insincere, and because, if it were sincere, it would be true to facts: for whereas you regard yourself as far greater than all, all as as far greater than you as you fancy them smaller, since your greatness is bedraggled rags that prevents you from being good. Oh, why are you not some ordinary wight, a young workman, Lepsius, a mason, a sailor, who has never learned to spell? Then some girl would so gleefully desert all her father's—— But now, ah, *il desir vive, e la speranza è morta*!... Do you, by the way, still believe it fine to steal?"

That this would give the profoundest offence Lepsius had no grounds to think, lying being to his philosophy no crime; but with that chastity of the swan, which, being but brushed in her array of whiteness, frills and ruffles awhile, then with majesty swims away, so she ruffled.

"Not 'frequently,' I think," Miss Eve repeated; "if I 'lie,' it is to myself, unwittingly; and in every event differ from you in fancying it 'fine.' Anyhow, now you can see how what you have wanted is out of the question."

At this Lepsius, looking at her under his eyes, said, "Eve, be sincere with me!"

She stopped, and he said, "I listen," but as she added nothing, he then said, "'Vulgar,' 'not Christian'; your criticism, of course, interests one, though it is curious."

"Tell me," Miss Eve said, "for whose weal do you purpose all that slaughter and upheaval—for the world's?"

"For my own," he said: "the weal of the world is in the management of the Genius-of-the-world, Who ceaselessly sees to it. I personally am not concerned in it."

"Then," replied Miss Eve, "that is what I mean by 'vulgar' and 'not Christian.'"

"One idea or two?" he asked.

"No, one."

Lepsius sat slowly aside on the bed, puzzling to understand her mind; and he said that he should have called Japan a far less 'vulgar' land than England, to which Miss Eve replied that if Japan was really the less vulgar, that could only signify that Japan was the more Christian.

"But if a million men are killed by it?" Miss Eve remarked.

"Dear, it will not matter," Lepsius replied.

"Will it matter if you are killed?"

"It will to you, to no one else, since everyone dislikes me."

"But *one* will clamour and cry out, you think? One will bleat and beat the breast?"

"Dear, it will not happen; I am so easily the king of men."

But here Lepsius stopped her with the whisper, "someone is coming!" on which the lips of Miss Eve, going at once quite sheet-white, breathed, "God! it must be my sister! Lepsius! go!"

"Why should I?" Lepsius said.

"Lepsius!"—she was beside herself—"would you compromise me? Lepsius? For ever? Would you?" for she herself could now catch the sound of something, a door moving open in an outer room.

"If I go," Lepsius whispered, "may I come every night?"

"Every——" Even in that storm of her eagerness for his going Miss Eve paused; but she breathed, "Yes, every night—the key!"

In an instant the key was handed her, and he out of the outer window: on which she, too, in some seconds was down, was across the bed and at the outer window, all her breath breathing down to him fifteen feet below, "Every night! But I shan't ever be here!"

She could just catch his ejaculation of "Wretch!" and as she snatched her fiddle, dashed herself into the chair at the casement, and arranged her drapery, soft footfalls came on the carpet, the elder sister breathing, "Eve! not in bed. Oh, Eve!"

"Dear," said Miss Eve with languor, "I couldn't get to sleep; I was playing the fiddle...."

"Well, I knew it.... I had a feeling that you were not asleep, so I got up and came to you, and here you are. Poor Evie! Cast your care upon God, will you, Eve?... But playing at this hour! And—where's the bow?"

"I put the bow over there.... Oh, Ruth, put your hand on my brow, I have a headache," upon which, her head now lying back on the chair-back, she shut down her eyelids, and Miss Ruth, stooping, held her hand over the brow of trouble, groaning now and again a little in her soul, her cheek pressed against Miss Eve's cheek, till presently she breathed, "That better now?"

"Yes, sweet, that's sweet," Miss Eve breathed.... "Sweet, Lepsius was here."

"Eve, here?"

And now, under the compulsion of that touch upon her brow, Miss Eve breathed out the whole story.

The sandals of Lepsius, meanwhile, were speeding away, till they arrived at his phaeton awaiting him beneath trees at Viroflay by the forest of Meudon, where, throwing himself in, under the setting moon he went tearing by way of Sèvres, Boulogne, Passy, to the palace. There, at the top of a stair, he was awaited by a man in robes of the Orient with a scraggy grey beard, hollow cheeks, and a nose mostly nostrils which gaped, who, with ever a wagging and nodding of his head, stood gossiping and gassing to Shan Healy: his name, Nundcumar. And these two, Shan Healy and Nundcumar, when Lepsius had mounted the stair, hastened without speech after their master's speed.

Perhaps a second lapsed before Nundcumar answered, "One: a person who can spangle silk-muslin with gold of Dacca for the women-folk."

"Tell! Man or woman?"

"It was a woman. She——"

"Name."

"I cannot at this moment remember her——"

"Tell! European?"

"Yes. She——"

Lepsius walked on; but after some steps, without stopping, went slower, and now beckoning Nundcumar to him, said low, "*You* walk before."

Nundcumar's eyes opened with some apprehension as he began to walk on ahead, and immediately Lepsius brought forth from the bag of his shirt a species of pigmy weapon which one fired off by pressure upon a button.

He then made his way to the place where he slept: an apartment as broad as the palace in that part, resembling a barn, but possessing no walls on three of its faces, only processions of columns of marble which bore up three architraves. Within this chamber a hound—a mastiff all but as large as Lepsius himself—was pacing about; and when Lepsius had well bolted four doors, had again loaded his weapon, had placed it on some straw strewn over one angle of the plain of floor, had let his gaze muse some moments upon the moon going down within a couch of clouds which she flushed, and now had thrown himself down upon the bed of straw, the hound moved to lie down by his side, and both soon dozed.

CHAPTER XII.

THE WEDDING-PLACE.

The day of the opening of the Exhibition was coming near, so was the day of the nuptials of Miss Eve and Monsieur de Courcy, which had first been fixed for the 23rd of July, and then, by the nerves and eagerness of the bride's groom and friends, fixed for the 5th; and now orders for the *gâteau de noce* and other articles had already gone out, and already the lady and her guardians were at Grönland, a seat of the Comtesse de Pichegru-Picard near to Orléans, where it was arranged that the marriage should take place.

In these circumstances Shan Healy observed truly to the Hindoo Nundcumar, "There be things brewing in his brain, as you'll see before too long—at work like six whirlwinds! And there's a little smile about'n somehow, and a something somewhere in his eye that spells pestilence to somebody, I haven't a doubt."

Healy was seated in the evening dusk by the Hindoo's side, who, still luxuriating in bed with his nose sore in cotton-wools, lay silent awhile, but then lifting himself to hug his meagre knees, said with that wagging of his head, "Let him run, let him go along; but one day the whirlpools of destiny will decapitulate his head."

"Oh, you go to hell," Healy muttered; "learn to speak Christian English first, and then turn prophet."

"Who's that, then?" Healy demanded, and the Hindoo's bony little face became animated a moment as he made answer, "The woman who threw the vitriol in my face!"

"Oh, she," said the other, "safe enough in chokey for four years anyway—'*travaux forcés*' they d' name it here; and serves her jolly well right, too."

Nundcumar, with his eyes shut and a head that wagged, said, "If she stops there!"

"Who's to get her out?" demanded Healy aggressively.

"I—do not know," remarked the Oriental innocently, with opening palms.

"Look here, you're a nice one to be speaking in this kind of way," Healy suddenly said; "appears to me as if you'd like to see it done!"

"Serves you right," observed Healy: "what earthly right had you to admit the woman into the palace without proper inquiries? And who was to have the vitriol in the chops, you or he, I should like to know?"

"He might have chosen *you* to have it," the Oriental quietly replied, throwing an underlook at Healy, upon which Healy chuckled within himself, saying, "Ey, but he didn't choose, you see!"

"No," said the Hindoo, "he chose his Nundcumar instead. But never mind, it's nothing, this. Only that's bad, Healy, my friend, when the evil eye is thrown upon a man, for there's not a god sitting on his throne of gold can escape——"

"And who's thrown this evil eye upon him?"

"That woman—that villain woman."

"Safe, thank God, under lock and key."

"May be; safe, thank God, under lock and key, may be: but did I never tell and expostulate you the history and anecdote of the time and epoch when I and my brother were in the service of the Maharajah of——"

"Do they believe *you*?" the Hindoo demanded; "may be I know one that doesn't, since he has had every step of yours spied, vigilised, and super-inspected ever since his sire has been over."

At this Healy, eyeing the floor, heaved a sigh, and then getting up from his seat, said with the dignity of grief, "Well, you are right there, no doubt," and walked out.

At that hour Lepsius himself, in an apartment without walls on a lower floor, was speaking with Mr. E. Reader Meade, who reposed on a couch at his ease, handing a moustache that rolled down like a weir, while Lepsius himself, in a sudeyree and trousers of nankeen, stood close to a telephone hung on one of the columns. In the midst a punkah, somehow worked, fanned the face; a fountain which span showered whirls of spray round flowers and ferns; two girls a good way off in corners continually caused their typewriters to prattle, peering nigh their work in the dusk; while here and there other species of machines competed in making their workings heard.

"Well," Mr. Reader Meade was saying in English, "their scheme of getting hold of your person, of course, seems to me, too, a bit absurd—and you say you knew of it?"

"Well?" said Lepsius to someone at the telephone, throwing immediately to Meade the reply, "Yes, I knew," and to the telephone-speaker the words, "Where, then, is Monsieur le Duc de Rey-Drouilhet at present?" and to Meade again, "Go on."

"I'll wait," said Meade.

"I listen," said Lepsius.

"Let us take it, then," said Meade, "that you will scarcely fail to elude that plot: for that's the sick spot of your Frenchman, he lacks humour, is so pre-occupied with *ideas*, that he lacks nice adjustment to facts, often fails to measure his new man or thing, and so comes a cropper in practice——"

"Precisely," said Lepsius, "you are very shrewd—as usual. Say then," he added to his telephone-speaker, "that I can receive Monsieur le Duc de Rey-Drouilhet for seven minutes."

"The castle to which you are to be inveigled," said Meade, "is called Château Egmond, on the Brittany coast, a league from St. Brieuc, and fourteen from your own Serapis. It is the property of Madame la Comtesse de Pichegru-Picard, has been leased from her by the League, I hear, and de Courcy, it is said, means to make it his residence immediately after his marriage, which takes place at Grönland, near Orléans, on the 5th—or am I giving you all stale news?"

"I knew," Lepsius said, as he now flew through the room to drop some words at the ear of one of the girls, who in turn eagerly spurted out; and now, returning, he said to Meade, seating himself on the floor with clasped knees, "Only I don't quite understand by what means they hope to get me to go to this Château Egmond."

Lepsius was up, speeding off to peer into a little machine hitched on to the telephone which fretted and roared in fits, saying as he ran, "But do they imagine that one cannot negotiate with Rémy, Schuré and Montijo without going down to Brittany? It is conspiracy of—let us say of Bismarcks, all born on the first of April!" at which word "Bismarcks" he chuckled maliciously within himself.

"But a conspiracy having this peril," remarked Meade, "that Isabeau Thiéry seems to be more or less in it."

"Oh, Thiéry is a shadow," said Lepsius, throwing himself flat on a table, his hands under his head; "his characteristic is that he does not exist."

"I should rather say," said Meade, "that his characteristic is that he is the half-brother of Fanny Schuré, who is the wife of Schuré, who is the engineer-in-chief of the moon-machine."

"And that matters in your judgment, I see," said Lepsius.

"You are always very shrewd," said Lepsius, lying on his back with shut eyes, "and but for your judgment I should surely miscarry in everything that I attempt. All this that you say is quite true, and I have always intended to bribe Isabeau Thiéry at the right moment."

"With money? Isabeau Thiéry?"

"Why the surprise?"

The Englishman got his limbs together, and sitting now on his couch-edge, stared, saying, "You cannot do that, you know.... Bribe any of them, the brokers, popes, emperors; but you cannot bribe a poet, man! Don't you know that for a fact, Lepsius? Frankly, you occasionally bring your friends' admiration of your brain to some sudden cropper...! You, too, having that French fixity of idea and lack of humour, knowing the human clock so minutely in everything, except just its divine trick, its 'eccentricity,' as mechanicians say. You couldn't bribe Thiéry!"

"Abundantly, I meant," observed Lepsius.

"But that's worse! If you send him five hundred francs, there's just the millionth fraction of a chance that it might influence him, since he is so jolly poor; but if you send him five millions, don't you know, really, what will happen? He'll throw up the melodramatic right-hand that crumples the cheque, cry 'Cato!' and rush off to Sister Fanny to crush you. It's the 'eccentricity' in the earth's yearly journey: you count ill if you leave it out."

At this Lepsius, springing up, looked at the other in the way of one who is struck by what has been said, and he had begun to say, "What grounds, now, have you——" when a negro, coming in between two of the columns, announced, "Monsieur le Duc de Rey-Drouilhet," and now Meade said, "Well, I'll be away," adding, "you can bribe *him*, Lepsius."

"And all of you," thought Lepsius within himself with a somewhat sullen eye askance on his friend.

The friendly Englishman and Lepsius, looking rather like cow and calf together, now exchanged a hand-shake, and in soon stepped the aged little duke, diffusing smells of perfumery, showing a youthful streak of teeth which shook, to seat himself finically on the couch which Meade had left, while anew Lepsius flew hither and thither, for some time paying no heed to the fop's presence, who meantime secretly touched his teeth, lips, cheeks, and sucked a cachou; till at last Lepsius, casting a look at one of a quartette of clocks, cheque-book in hand, dashed to sit by his side, remarking, "Six minutes and a half, Monsieur le Duc, and my admirable friend: tell."

"Why, it was you who sent for me," the duke said, tittering in his fluttering and fussy manner, "it is you, Monsieur Lepsius, whose rôle it is to tell!"

To this Lepsius made no answer, but stamping a cheque with a number of francs, furiously wrote the duke's name on it, and now threw the cheque askew to the duke's knees, without looking at him; upon which the duke sprang up somewhat pallid under his rouge, muttering in a protesting manner, "No, Monsieur Lepsius—your manner—I cannot accept—you forget, monsieur——"

Lepsius groaned. "We are such old cronies! And surely time is ever a thing of some value. Can you *not* see it? Tell, tell."

"I am aware that your time is valuable——"

"Yes, of course: tell."

"But——"

"No, tell."

"But are there to be no preliminaries? No pourparlers? You have handed me a cheque, monsieur—I know not for what amount, since positively I decline to inspect it——"

"Twenty thousand, that being the first of several, the others to be written out as you proceed in amounts proportioned to the worth of your words."

"The figures will be big in that event!"

"They shall be; you know that I am immense in generosity."

"But it is a bribe!—if you consider it. I was never, however, to be bribed! You forget, monsieur, that I bear a name which I never have, nor ever shall, stain by any real meanness; nor, if I have accepted money of you in the past——"

"It was not a bribe, it was a gratuity; a meanness, but not a 'real' meanness, because of your secret ardour for my person and service. I know it all, nor should ever dream of insulting that name you bear with a 'real' bribe: tell."

"Well, provided we do thoroughly understand each other's tone, monsieur ..." the duke now said, sitting down anew with a twitching up of his trousers' knees, "though in the present instance I absolutely do not feel that I could touch your cheque with honour, since, really, if you consider it, monsieur, it is a betrayal of comrades, this, in which I am engaged—you cannot get rid of the fact by any sophistry!—it—is—a—betrayal; nothing less!"

"Not a betrayal, only an exposure," said Lepsius drearily, "nor need you actually touch the cheque," and picking it up, he put it into the peer's pocket.

"Well, say an 'exposure,' since everything, after all, depends on the tone of an act, and everything is right that is done by the right-minded.... At any rate, let me tell you, monsieur, that you stand in a situation of even the extremist danger!"

"I know; and Isabeau Thiéry is in it."

"Why, yes."

"Tell—deeply?"

"Deeply enough, although not whole-heartedly, I know. Moreover, he hasn't a sou, so can at any moment be opened to you by the golden key."

"And Dr. Lepsius?"

"He also ... I am in the dark, by the way, as to whether the doctor is a relative of yours, although the question is being asked——"

"No relative. But that man is actually in the inside of the inner plot to kidnap and imprison me? Yes?"

"Why, yes. He has attended each of the recent councils in the house of Monseigneur Piscari, has even made suggestions as to the means of your capture."

The answer was, "Yes."

"Telephone to P.," said Lepsius, "asking if all is ready on his side, in which case let him now wire to B13 to burn within an hour." At the same time, without looking round, he cried out to the duke, "You see the amount is as I stated it, Monsieur le Duc!" for the duke was taking the chance to scrutinise his cheque narrowly in the twilight.

"I will see to it," was the answer of the speaking-tube to Lepsius, who then sped back to the duke, saying, "Two minutes more, monsieur; tell details."

The old fop laid one forefinger on the other, and with much animation of manner gave the details. Lepsius was to be got to Château Egmond, a league from St. Brieuc, by means of an accumulation of inducements, the chief being that Schuré, the engineer, without speaking with whom it was assumed that Lepsius could not exist a week, would be present: for Schuré, though not of the conspiracy—at all events not formally, so far—had, however, promised to be of the house-party for two or three days; and it was proposed that Schuré should fall more or less indisposed while there through unwholesomeness in his wine for, at any rate, eight or nine days, until Lepsius should be impelled to hie to his bedside. Then Lepsius was to be shut up in the château some days, until he could be taken to the bastille on the Ile de Bas, named Château Labîme, which, too, the League had got on lease; and it was moreover hoped to reduce Lepsius to penury by seizing a minute key which Lepsius was believed to carry continually on his body.

"Their names," said Lepsius, smiling a little, toying under his vest with that half a coin whose sister-half he had sent to Miss Eve Vickery two years previously.

"The provincials," said the duke, "are obscure rich persons, not worth your resentment, monsieur; there is a Monsieur Louis Jammes of Lyons, a chocolate-maker, then a Monsieur Flammarion of Tours, a Monsieur Brisson of Rouen—who, by the way, is booked to go to the conference at Château Egmond."

"I do not know these people," remarked Lepsius with no little alertness of thought in his eyes which stirred fleetly from side to side like sheet-lightning. He then asked if the provincials had attended the Paris conferences, to which the other replied that they had not, being but "associates" by correspondence with Sauriau, their secretary.

As he departed, Lepsius threw half a look at one of four clocks, their staring faces of a largeness so exaggerated that they concealed, each of them, four of the columns' mass, and afflicted the air with the click of their tick-tack; and with one tap of impatience on a chair he went muttering, "Come, Sauriau."

Some seconds afterwards the name of the Abbé Sauriau was called.

"Admit him!" called Lepsius in reply, at the same time darting behind a screen, whence in scarce more than forty seconds he came out "dressed" in clothes made for quickness, without any buttons about them, and a second before the abbé came in had caught up, and was casting his eye over, a page of a book of the abbé's just published.

"Monsieur l'Abbé Sauriau," he murmured, shaking hands, "I was at this moment deep in *Hellenic Idylls....* But what are you, then, Monsieur l'Abbé Sauriau. A re-incarnation of Plato? For surely, only a Greek could so utterly know the soul of Greece!"

Monsieur l'Abbé Sauriau had shy eyelids. "I am glad.... Ah! you have seen *Hellenic Idylls.*"

"Seen and devoured ... and what charm! How airy! What daintiness of manner! Oh, truly, those gross fingers of the Abbé Sauriau know how to engrave with a fairy's grace."

"Why, this is well," said the abbé; "have you, by chance—finished the book?"

"Not quite, yet, monsieur: I am now at the myth of Leda."

"It is the end that is the best," breathed the abbé with downbent lids.

Lepsius, who did not much care, leapt up just then to answer the telephone, and before he came back to the abbé peered into the machine in which a château was slowly painting its shape on a pane of paper: upon which his visitor called to him, "What a fuss of mechanism you have squalling in this hall!"

"Come, I'll let you see them," said Lepsius in a humour of devilry, to humiliate the spirit that he had lately praised; and he led the priest from little machine to little machine, teaching him something of the meaning of each—things of steel acting in the manner of rational and ingenious creatures—into which those bushy eyes of the Abbé Sauriau peered near-sightedly, and though he uttered hardly a word, from time to time a "humph!" would start from him. When, however, they came to the one where the château was coming out in colours, Lepsius nonchalantly said,

"This one you could not comprehend, however much I explained it," and dropped a handkerchief on it.

In this manner, half by carelessness, half in malice, he made for himself many enemies, by contempt; and in the abbé's eyes came a flame.

Lepsius span round to the abbé, saying, "I wonder?... Whereabouts?"

"The name is Château Egmond——"

"I didn't know that the prelate had a palace of that name."

"He has lately taken it on a——"

"Where is it?"

"In Brittany, not twenty leagues from your own Palace Serapis, and a league from——"

"Ah, too far. Time, Monsieur l'Abbé," and off Lepsius dashed anew to the machine of the château-picture, snatched the handkerchief from it, peered, and now beheld midget people rushing about it, and the château at four places wrapt in flames; upon which he flew back to the abbé, who was observing, "Well, certainly, it is a long way off, but then everywhere is near to Dædalus; moreover, everybody will be there—Schuré, Montijo—many charming dames——"

"Ah! Who, for instance?"

"Madame Schuré for one," replied the abbé with a flash of the eye.

"Unfortunately, monsieur," remarked Lepsius very rashly, "I can't be expected to make love to a *rat d'opéra* like Fanny Schuré when it is well known that I am already in love, and with a sovereign lady. If, now, you had informed me that the Comtesse de Pichegru-Picard and her charming relatives would be there, that to a great extent would have abolished the distance."

The abbé sat up at this, staring like one who is struck by a new idea, then muttered with some spite, "I was wondering if that could be managed, just to please you. It seems, however, to be out of the question, since one of those relatives of the countess is to be married on the 5th to Monsieur de Courcy at Grönland, in the centre."

"And Monsieur de Courcy has not asked me to be a guest!" crowed Lepsius with gross sarcasm, adding, "Forgive me—forty seconds," and anew he flew to the machine of the château-picture, a "living" picture, in which could be seen the leaping of flames that now surrounded all the place, and crowds rushing all about, and fire-engines spouting out waters in the night, all such mites as are the images which walk tiny in the eye of an ox. Lepsius gazed at it through a magnifying-glass, and when in a group of eight moving down a terrace in disarray from the house of flame he could make out the faces and shapes of the Misses Vickery, back he rushed to the abbé, saying, "That, then, must be my answer, Monsieur l'Abbé, to Monseigneur Piscari, with my thanks; nor will anything earthly alter my decision—unless, perhaps, it be some temptation in the shape of the eternal feminine.... You see, Monsieur l'Abbé, I become dissipated in mind like the rest, and oh, believe me, it is a relaxing thing to live among men.... What's the time?"

It was the home of the Count de Courcy. The count, however, was out, but might be found, the abbé was told, at the Ministère, or else at a house in the Rue du Faubourg St. Honoré.

To the Ministère drove the abbé; no de Courcy was there; so thence he drove to the Faubourg, where the Comte de Courcy rose from dinner to go to him at the head of a stair, and there the abbé said, with a scantness of breath, "I have been chasing you—am fresh from the individual whom—that is, from the young Lepsius, and shall be surprised from his mood at present if anything which we can devise will get him to step into the Egmond trap.... Would you believe? he is love-struck with *Hellenic Idylls*; it appears, my friend, that the young man dreams of it at night!"

"*C'est vrai?*" said Monsieur de Courcy (i.e., "By Jove," touched with irony).

"Yes, you will find him turning author before long in order to vie with us others! But, believe me, monsieur, he is destined to discover that it needs a deeper brain to create a true and poetical book than to imagine machines of steel."

"As Phœbus beats Hephæstus; but—you see—I am being await- ed——"

"Yes, forgive me—only to tell you that it will be most difficult, as I can already see, to get him to go to Egmond, unless—may I express my- self? it is delicate...."

"I even pray you to do so."

"Unless Madame de Pichegru-Picard and her—nieces are of the party, in which event he will agree——"

The Comte de Courcy's neck stiffened. "My friend, the suggestion would be ingenious, if it were not impossible."

"I see that," breathed the Abbé Sauriau, "especially its ingeniousness."

"To me its impossibility is no less obvious, monsieur," said Monsieur de Courcy.

But now steps were mounting the stair, and a man bearing a document and a telegram came up to give them to the count, who, having read the telegram, grew pale, and every second paler, and presently observed to the abbé, "My God! Grönland house burned to the ground!"

"Burned!" exclaimed the abbé; "why, accept my sym—— But where, then, monsieur, will your wedding take place?"

"It may now *have* to be at Egmond," the count said slowly, with meditation dwelling in his underlook.

"Why, then, this may be a Providence in view of the individual whom we have in our mind!" cried out the Abbé Sauriau.

"We will see how Heaven works it," the count observed, now suddenly holding out his hand to bid *bon soir*.

CHAPTER XIII.

Within ten days everything was settled: the Comtesse de Pichegru-Picard, burnt out of Château Grönland, came to an arrangement with Monseigneur Piscari (who had already got from her the lease of Egmond in Brittany on behalf of the League), to go down there for the wedding of Miss Eve without interfering with the prelate's house-party; and Lepsius, for his part, on hearing now that Miss Eve would be at Egmond, agreed to go down, too, to meet the other political intriguers.

By the last day of June all the party were there, except a Monsieur Brisson of Rouen, and Lepsius, who had arranged to come on the 2nd of July for two days, the date of the wedding remaining fixed for the 5th of July.

As for this Monsieur Brisson, who lived not far from Brittany, why he did not appear was not very clear, for though he had been written to by Monseigneur Piscari, he had sent no reply.

The difficulty was to get Lepsius into Egmond without scandal: for if he once came in as a guest, and was seen, his disappearance would naturally excite comment and unrest; but after much discussion one Captain Pertius, a spark of the *beau sabreur* type, who had five *pioupious* (privates) at command in the château, proposed that as Lepsius came, his capture should take place outside a summer-house in a south avenue, and Lepsius there kept till everybody was abed; and this was carried.

But now Monsieur Brisson of Rouen, with a rasping throat of the *nouveau riche*, at last gave a croak, saying, "It will be a great risk to keep him idling there for hours in that summer-house."

And now, too, for the first time, Dr. Lepsius breathed a weary word, "I agree."

However, their votes were overborne on the authority of Pertius, who, having thoroughly examined the summer-house, had found it strong and sound.

"It was Captain Pertius," said Monseigneur Piscari.

"And you have all inspected it?" asked Monsieur Brisson.

"Most of us," remarked Monsieur de Courcy; "it is a good, good place, monsieur."

"It may be good," said Monsieur Brisson, "but is it the best? Oh, believe me, messieurs, in everything there is a bad, a good, a better, and a best, the best ever more grievous than the rest, but so greatly better than the better."

"True," murmured the Abbé Sauriau: "*is* it the best?"

"I propose that we search the château in a body first," suggested Monsieur Brisson.

After all, it was found that the tower-chamber which Captain Pertius had chosen was the most eligible; and, everything at last arranged, the committee separated to come among the ladies.

At this hour, with the moon in the clouds, and groups of ladies and their gallants moving round the grounds, and sounds of music in the *salons* and galleries, Egmond looked a stately and picturesque place. The Misses Vickery were strolling with Monsieur de Courcy along the brink of an oblong of water that stretched far-slumbering in boscage from the bottom of the terraces to a mosque of marble at its far end, when there came up to them Dr. Lepsius to take part in their walk; but presently a messenger from Monseigneur Piscari came to call Monsieur de Courcy, who with his lips just touched a finger-tip of his future-one with a great parade of grace, and went away; soon after which Miss Ruth, too, was called by another party of promenaders—a Schuré group, Fanny Schuré burnished in coloured fires like mother-of-pearl, with whom Miss Ruth stopped to gossip, the innocent with the guilty, Dr. Lepsius and Miss Eve meantime going on to the mosque.

Miss Eve had risen, seeming in her white evening-dress, with whitest cheeks, even weird in that sheen, and she replied with a chuckle, "It was prophesied me that I should not be a bride for some time to come!"

"By my son?... Well, he has no little might in this lower world," the old man murmured, "but have no fear, he is by no means omnipotent, and, as I have hinted, he is at this moment in extreme peril for his own skin."

Sharply at this, with a haughty heave-up of her chin, Miss Eve asked, "Who could touch him?"

"Ah! it is dubious," the old man said musingly, bending over his oak stick; "still—I believe—by many eyes, and by many hands, and by the agreement of many wits and wills of men and God, it shall be achieved!" and now he struck the stick sharply upon the *perron* of steps down which they were now passing to the path, Miss Eve laughing a little with a meaning that was hardly understood, saying, "And his father, if I am rightly informed, is with his enemies?"

"That is so," said Dr. Lepsius with an inclination of his head, whereat she stopped walking to face him, asking, "With your eyes quite open, Dr. Lepsius?"

"Well, I hope so," the doctor answered.

"You have thought, then, of what will certainly happen, if—after—I am married on Friday?"

Dr. Lepsius glanced up at her, having noted her tones go shaky, and on beholding her face bony with agitation, said with some astonishment, "No, what will happen?"

"Your son will *kill* himself."

And while the doctor with an eye of scare stared at her, she with a certain roistering and hilarity added, "And since royalty should have servants rejoicing to join in its voyages, *two* you may see, if not more, go to attend on his ghost."

"Two—I do not quite——" the doctor stammered.

"I meant my poor father for one," she sighed, continuing to walk.

But since her "kill himself" the doctor had but absently heard what was said, and "kill himself!" he cried suddenly, crimson with anger, "let him! let him! I will go to his funeral! For I'd sooner follow him to the tomb——"

"Now, Dr. Lepsius, a father ought not to be down on a son," Miss Eve said, "though I know that he has been beastly to you."

At this tears gushed to the old man's eyes. "Oh, it isn't that, dear Eve—it isn't the bitter ingratitude, the bruise, the gash in here: but how shall I not be against him in what he undoubtedly aims to bring about, when the mouth of every gash which he gives our race will shout out in rage against me? You see, do you not——?"

It was Monsieur Brisson of Rouen.

And when Miss Eve looked at him without seeming to know him, he, though undoubtedly agitated, said with a coarse chuckle that she and he had been shoulder to shoulder at the Quai d'Orsay that evening when a particular individual had dared to take a liberty with her lips: at which

thing Miss Eve stood like a queen who stands astonished at so much inso-
lence under the sun, then silently went on her way.

But this Monsieur Brisson was not one who could be banished with a
chin; he followed to breathe near Miss Eve's ear, "I wish to speak to you
of him, he may be here to-morrow, and I have a message...."

"*Here?*"

"Let us go down that *allée*."

She hesitated, and he glanced like lightning at his watch. "Only three
minutes to be with you—come."

Now she walked with him into the dark of the *allée*, looking down at
the ground, like one magnetised, drawn with a cord.

"For what reason will he be here?" she breathed.

"On business."

"You are to inform your master, monsieur," she then said in a haughty
manner, "if Monsieur Lepsius happens to be your master, that I know him
to be in much danger, so that he should have a care."

"This instant?" she whispered furtively: "to fly? Away? With you?...
But what, then, am I? A beast, with a beast's soul? Evil to the core? Reck-
less, furious, moon-struck? Is there no Christ for me on high, I wonder?
No right? No wrong?"

"If you came," said her companion with some bitterness, though
touched by her trouble, "it would save much time; and you would come,
if hypocrisy was not your breath and bread," upon which she rushed into
an irritation not to be restrained, crying, "That is monstrously untrue and
unkind! I mean well!"

"Well," he said, "I did not expect you to come with me, for I know
you. But you have to show me the windows of your bed-chamber."

Now she stopped walking, standing tall, gaunt, her heart galloping up
in her gorge, asking, "Why my windows?"

"Oh, nothing: just show," he muttered; and when she had stared a little
while at him, she paced on in silence.

She, with her back toward the house and toward him, her brow bent
downward, replied to the ground in a proud guttural that trembled, "I am
sure I do not know why such a question should be asked of me.... My
windows happen to be those two on the first floor immediately over the

balcony-end near by the statue—since it seems that the knowledge is desired."

The plash of the coat with its weight sounded now in the lake, and "Monsieur Brisson," that bow of his right leg quite gone, stood now limber on his bare feet, his elbow suddenly about Miss Eve's waist: whereat she, feeling his lips stealing near her face, went fearfully pale; nearer, and she shivered with sickness; nearer, and she sucked in her breath as at luscious juice and shooting pangs, sighed "By heaven," and had his lips.

He put her to lie on a bench of marble by the waterside, whence she through her half-shut eyelids watched him run away with a deer's ease up an avenue of the park, and disappear in darkness.

On the day commencing to dim, he took out his collar-stud, touched it, and it shed round his sheets an electric sheen.

Soon after two in the morning he was removed to the room fitted out for him in the tower; the same hour the members of the League being met in council to congratulate each other and resolve on the next measures.

Lepsius, however, was there in the tower, safe enough, which was everything.... It was an eight-cornered chamber where he was, arranged with some little luxury, and large; but he suffered, being unaccustomed to be between walls, and here was but one window, with bars in it, while, as to the lush carpet, the eye of his consciousness was at every moment open to the microbic hordes that must be at barracks within it, nor could he bathe with ease, he who bathed frequently each day, nor was the food such as was usual with him, being much too luscious.

This was first served to him by a person who had a beard and appeared to be a man, but was not so loosely costumed but that certain curves of the womanly could be observed in him—or her. On seeing her when she bore in his breakfast, Lepsius moaned, and flew to the other extremity of the chamber, where he held a chair-back, ready if she attacked; but when she had put down the breakfast without glancing at him, and had gone, his brow reddened, and having begged one of four guards for pen and ink, he wrote to Monseigneur Piscari, asking whether monseigneur was privy to the fact that one Jeanne Auvache, a convict with a mania, who had been aided by his, Lepsius', enemies, to evade prison, had been sent to attend upon him. He received no answer to this, but the woman ceased to appear at meals.

He knew (having been at the council), that at the hour of two he was to be roused to go on board a brig, bound for the bastille on the Ile de Bas; so he had commanded Shan Healy to conceal himself in the château and come to the prison-door exactly at 1.50, so as to help Lepsius to carry a load which Lepsius conceived that he would have need to carry. Ten minutes, then, before that 1.50, at a moment when preparations were being made in the château below to take him to the ship, Lepsius awoke to act. He was still at the lock of the door with the two little tools that he had hidden in the summer-house before his capture, when howls of "Help! help!" broke out without the door, and he was made aware that Shan Healy must be engaged in a struggle with the greenhorn *pioupiou* on guard out there; but the *pioupiou's* howls were at once drowned in the sound of a disturbance resembling the bursting of some tremendous drum somewhere, which just then made the château to tremble through its breadth and length; and before that roaring was well over, Shan, who had felled the *pioupiou* with the *pioupiou's* lantern, broke blithely with the lantern-light into the room, the lock of whose door had at that moment opened to the key of Lepsius.

He could not help shrieking...!

"Idiot!" hissed Lepsius, who, as he now darted away, caught a weapon out of Shan's pocket, sent with one glance backward and a nervous gurgle of chuckling a bullet into the woman's bosom, which, however, chanced not to end her, and was out and away.

Erect on her bare soles in an alcove, robed in a bedroom-robe of lace, a stone stone-still, her hair a rope plaited to a bow of ribbon at her knees, Miss Eve stood, waiting, aware of his tumults, but beauteously dead, as one who has interviewed the stare of Medusa; and all in a tick, like a cat fawning, Lepsius was cast at her feet, kissing them, pleading, "Dear, will you come with me?"

Her friends were pressingly clamouring at the entrance; they screamed, "*Eve!*"

She took no notice of them, if she heard; as to Lepsius, she hurled up her right hand to strike him dead, crying, "You brute!"

"Oh, do—for us two—beloved——"

"I bitterly hate and abhor the pair of us!"

"But you will get us both killed——"

"Thank God!"

Southward, a smoke that soared to the clouds was being poured out steadily from the château, which ever throed inwardly with loud-bursting noises and sounds of rumbling like poisoned bowels and Etna boiling; and that plume of fume-and-fire slanted continually from point to point of the compass, for a wind boisterously blew, drizzle sprayed the face, and the moon, while suffusing the night wildly with the whiteness of her light, was herself quite hidden away out of sight in cloud.

Lepsius was soon up and gone again with his load, knowing that pursuit would not be slow: but it was a great labour; the country there is rugged; Miss Eve, drugged, could not, or would not, keep on her feet; Healy, with whose help the load would have been easy, moaned in his agonies somewhere; and the bay lay nearly a league away.

They lodged her, still unconscious (as it seemed), among cushions, and plied to the ship, which, lying with steam at a moment's notice, immediately steamed away, turning toward the west: and rushing she went, urgently churning the sea—a long boat burnished with Tobin-bronze, burning the eye like a strip of the sun; and as the dawn worked and began gradually to overspread all the world of waters and of coast, Lepsius, prying a port on the stern, spied like pearl the pinnacles of Serapis.

CHAPTER XIV.

AT SERAPIS.

Lepsius, to the amazement of men, remained at Serapis for weeks, to the very eve of the Exhibition, though he quickly established a system of posts and telephones with Monsieur Schuré and other men of importance: as to which the Hindoo, Nundcumar, remarked to Shan Healy, "It is a piece of slackness, this; once he would not have done this: but when a woman comes in, great minds begin to go rotten, and look a little ahead, my sonnies, and you will see their catastrophe head-over-heels."

It was then the turn of the Hindoo with his burned nose to drone by the bedside of Healy; and Healy, who had conceived a fever from his vitriol-dose, said with a moan, "Won't she let him see her yet?"

Shan Healy tossed for ease, moaning. "Anybody can easy enough guess out what was in it; but how the deuce do *you* know?"

"I know and I know," said the Hindoo with a moving head, "and what I do not know is what man knoweth not, for that which is is shown unto me. And in the note, word for word, she says, 'Lepsius, I admit myself your prisoner here in Serapis. You understand though, I think, knowing me armed, that I instantly die if you venture to enter anew any part of my palace; test me, I woo you, to see whether I mean it or not.—EVE.' That was her scribble, my sonnies, and the wording and reverbosity of her constructing."

Healy opened and closed anew his sick eyes to reply, "*If* it's true."

"What, don't you suppose I ever let slip something that's true, for form's sake, in the hey-day and prime of life?" prated the utterly senseless ape-tongue of the Hindoo that ambled blandly in a monotone along, with the obscurest meanings anon, if meaning it had.

"So he ain't seen her since?" Healy asked.

"He has seen her every day, though she little thinks it! for she is artful, but he is artfuller still——"

"Old gas-bag," Healy moaned, "you said just now that *he* is artful, but *she* is artfuller still."

"Both are artfuller than each one, my chum Healy," Nundcumar said: "*he* is artfuller than she because he is of the guiley ones and artful dodges, the beguilers and the wilers, and *she* is artfuller than he because she is a woman, and the guilt of womanhood is in the juice of her gall-bladder. But he sees her when she little believes it: his eyes have their peep-holes and their spy-places to weigh her and dwell upon her when she's wantoning on the water with her poet and her ladies, or when she is walking under the arcade of the courtyard gazing at the gauderies and the graces of her Persian and Delhi girls dancing with their carcanets of pearl in the moonshine: for she grows every day more luxuriatingous, which is the curse of Serapis for everyone who enters it, from the lord of all to the low-cast coolie who polishes the porphyries; and in these three weeks she has grown into a regular begum-queen, true-blue old England as she is, and if he only waits a bit, he will get and win her, be certain—that is, if she does not flirt off abscond and run away first with the young poet Pershorez——"

At this the sick man looked at Nundcumar to sigh, "Oh, you scandalous tongue—if I only had the strength——"

"Why, my friend Healy," said Nundcumar, "have your ears not heard how she pets her little Pershorez? Cannot stir without him near her! Feeds him with sweetmeats, conserve of roses, orange-honey of Kauzeroon, and all delights, almond-patés, and amusements! her eyes musing on his eyes all an afternoon in that small hall of red andem-wood, while he recites to her from Hafez and Ferdousi, sir-poets of Persia whom she cannot understand a word, though she can well understand the face of Pershorez, my sonnies, which is only made of cream of gazelle-milk and rose-leaves fading, and his little figure more perfect in grace, symmetry, curves, and very hungriness of perfecting than Thammuz, the love-god that Syrian girls go thin for fancy of, and sigh for very hungriness of delight, and die of. And that other one, the lord of all, he knows, he knows, of this, because Barova, the little Arab slave-maid, who is thin, faint and gaunt for love of lord Lepsius, she pushed her way one night right into his private hall in the north palace, and told out of her mistress, how the grossness of the sap of womanly hungriness grows wanton in the arteries of her gall for Pershorez; and first he could not grasp what the girl wished to say to him, but then for very anguish of jealousy he cast back his head-piece and laughed wild——"

"Laughed for fun," sighed Healy—"if any of it is true."

The sick fellow whined at this, sighing, "Pity you're quite so vile an old liar, after all."

Here, however, the entrance of a sister-of-mercy, Healy's nurse, whose frown the Hindoo knew, interrupted and drove him out; immediately whereupon Healy begged to be permitted to pen a note, and on gaining the battle, wrote as follows: "Master Hanni, I beg to be forgiven for writing to you, but as I do not much fancy now that I shall ever be getting up out of this again, that's why I take this liberty, which is to say that I wish to God, Master Hanni, you would get that dog of a Hindoo Nundcumar from being near about you, for he means you no good, I doubt, and under the ridiculousness of a parrot this man hides ten times the craftiness of a fox. Dear Master Hanni, you may not be aware that thirteen years since Nundcumar was two years in Wormwood Scrubbs Prison, near by London, for stealing two bicycles. And, Master Hanni, that you may never cease to remember with any breath you breathe that Jeanne Auvache remains alive is the dying prayer of yours till death, Shan Healy. I'd give fifteen years, if I had fifteen days, to lay my eyes on your face once again for one moment on this side, but that may be a bit more than I can expect of you: and, if not, good-bye to you."

"Not so, monsieur, I think," said Monsieur Hugonnet, a big bureaucrat, who ever struck the wind with his eye-glass in his fingers: "that theory is no longer tenable, for it is now established that some shreds of her body must have been found. Moreover, you do not forget the crew of the brig's boat who saw a lady carried into your boat?"

"It was another lady," replied Lepsius, smiling, "as ten days ago I gave myself the pains to prove to Monsieur Leflô and Lord Rawlinson."

"Monsieur, I admit it," the commissary replied: "you have conclusively proved that Miss Vickery is made of air; this, nevertheless, seems a matter in which frankness, reasonableness and right feeling might well be invoked on both sides. Think, monsieur—the lady's father lies half dead of it; and the English Government, I give you my word, monsieur, grows every day more earnest, more urgent——" at which Lepsius, jumping up with a rather reddened brow, went walking about a hall all pillars of marble, between which stretched screens of perforated marble and filigrees of gold, screens low enough for one to overgaze, away below, the crags of the Brittany coast, and, away beyond these, a streak of sea, indigo corruscated with snow-glints under the sun's glare.

"Serapis is not so much a palace as a town——" the commissary commenced to say.

"Still, you have searched it throughout!"

"Let us search it again, monsieur, for certainty's sake!"

"Again? And when?"

"Say to-morrow, will you?"

"Well, it is ridiculous; still——"

"Scribble me a pass, monsieur!"

Lepsius scribbled a pass for the following day, and the commissary went away.

As for Lepsius, he had no fear of the legal visit, since his reason for giving Miss Eve her (west) palace was that in it were rooms so curiously and astutely concealed, that no keenest wit could suspect them; and on the previous visit of the police Miss Eve was easily induced on some excuse to step, unsuspecting, into one of these. So Lepsius smiled, as he once more stepped up to recline in his kind of throne, little thinking that that commissary was more cunning than he looked.

Lepsius stood about two minutes, looking down at that rash on the sick brow, the bandages on the breached cheek; took up, looked at, smelled two of the medicine bottles; took up and held the sick hand; and, holding it, gazed out with a brow of trouble through a great window which was hollowed out in Moorish ogives, out into a court where the whiteness of a minaret in the midst of a lake was reflected far down in the water, with zephyrs flirting along the water's surface: an afternoon in July in which all that Brittany country slumbrously basked, and bumblebees, as air-boats trading, tromboned a moment, as through steamboat throttles, their boom of music across the ear-drum dreamily, and cruised to some other ear. Somehow Lepsius sighed. And whispering the sister, "Tell him that I came," he went away in haste.

But he had hardly passed beyond the door's hanging, when a French functionary with a wild and white face, wringing his hands together, raced to him with the hiss, "My God, monsieur, all is lost! Monsieur Hugonnet has gained admission with a squad of gendarmes, and is now searching Miss Vickery's house!"

Lepsius flew....

Not toward the west palace, but back toward his own north, and not the way he had come, but as the bird flies, one eye on the watch on his palm, one on the way he went, once swinging over a wall, once swimming an oval of water, trampling flower-beds, routing men, making one bound of stairs, while the fowls of the air cried out their affright at his flight; and now like whirlwind his fingers were scattering among masses of trinkets and things in a certain mahogany, he groaning in his soul; got what he wanted; and now was gone again, going straight as the bird goes, west and south, swinging, swimming, bounding, and now at last was in the south-west house.

Some seconds later Monsieur Hugonnet and his troop rapped, came in, inspected the group of Oriental maids, the poet (lone male among women) with his lute, the gazelle, and the old Ulema, Imam or Cadi taking siesta on the yatag in his turban, softly fanned by his girls. The gendarmes cast glances at the group of girls—could hardly be got to move on; but presently searched through the hall, and spent the rest of the day in searching Serapis in vain.

Nor did Monsieur Hugonnet go out as he came in. In passing down a stair in the north palace, he and several of his men slipped down it, three spraining their legs; in one place he got an electric stroke; and in his going out of Serapis a grate gave way under him—a grate that had sustained all his men—nor was it without difficulty that he was raised up, half-drowned in filth, out of a drain.

"Alone?" said he, with his elbows laid on a table to stare at her paled face upon which a lamp shone, she seated with her luggage (a hand-bag) at her feet, a pretty sprig in her hat, for she liked little fineries and vanities, provided they were very cheap.

"Yes," she replied to him, "quite alone."

"You have come to see—Serapis?"

"Why, what a question—for Eve!"

"If I had Eve, do you imagine that I should give her to you?"

"I am even sure that you will, if I beg you."

"Beg me, and see."

"You admit, then, that you have her.... Tell me whether she is well!"

"No, she is not in Serapis. I fancy I know where she might be traced, but she is not in Serapis."

"Oh, fie, you tell lies; why, I have seen her here."

"You?"

"Yes, three afternoons ago, in a dream. I hardly ever go to sleep in the day-time, but somehow that afternoon about two sleep overpowered me, and Eve lay before my feet. She lay asleep, and she was an old man with a beard somehow, and yet she was Eve, and a goat with its forelegs doubled underneath it fed by her feet, and it was here in Serapis, I knew very well, in a room with a dome over it."

Lepsius, staring at her, remained dumb.

"So you see," she remarked with an underlook, "there are more kingdoms than you have visited."

"Myriads more," he mumbled.

"Have you married her, may I ask?"

He, his gaze on the table, mumbled, "If I even go near her, she raises a dagger to pierce her bosom."

"Good old Eve," breathed Miss Ruth, staring in surprise; but added immediately with veiled eyes, to soothe the agonies which she guessed, "that is not because she loves anyone less, but because she loves God more."

"You are an unintelligible family," he remarked with half a shrug.

"Oh, but well-meaning, I think, well-wishing," she said. "Anyway, if—since—she may not come with me, I will stay with her."

"No; if you stay, you stay a captive; and, if I allow you to, I thereby avow that Eve is here."

"No one will know but my papa, who promises you, if you will let me be with her, never to tell anyone."

"So, then," asked Lepsius, "you imagine me sufficiently childish to rely upon your father's promise?"

"You do not? Really? How curious! Well, *I* undertake, then——"

"Your undertaking is without weight. Moreover, you once before broke a promise that you made me."

"When?"

"At The Towers, as to betraying my presence to Dr. Lepsius...."

"Oh, but if one meant well! Look, now, into one's eyes...."

Then he said, "But you are all against me; you would be speaking against me to Eve."

"Well, then, I will undertake never again to do that."

"That is not enough; I say no, unless you will undertake to woo her in my favour."

"Now, how can I? Is she not affianced to——?"

"How laughable!" shouted Lepsius: "she shrieks with laughter at the mere thought of such a farce! De Courcy is a gnat, a limpet in a hag of peat-water! And since you, meaning well, could break your promise made to me, why may not Eve, meaning well, break her promise made to this ape-man?"

"Oh, I," Miss Ruth replied with her touch of flippancy, "I'd crash through a promise like piecrust any day, if I saw fit, for I think that a Christian is set free from rules, and in the pure every crime is pure. My sister, however, regards herself as more bound by laws and modes, and as to departing from a promise once given, it has always been her way, I know, to regard that as rather a ghastly business. But suppose that somehow the fact of her espousal could be overcome, how can I ever possibly cry back to your cause, knowing that you are not a Christian?"

Lepsius smiled. "If that be all, regard the knot of Gordium as cut: I become a Christian this night."

"How will you—'this night'?"

"Isn't there something about being plunged into holy water?"

"To be plunged into holy water is hardly to be a Christian, I think."

"What, then, is?"

"To wish well to the world, I think; to live to serve it; to stand piously alert to suffer and die for it"—with down-turned lids she uttered this, and, as he heard it, his brow twitched once; then bringing his mouth down to the table, he mumbled, as it seemed, to nobody, "A lady here to be led away west," and as a guard in gauds appeared, he remarked to Miss Ruth, "You will hardly be able to persuade me that you are a thinker, you know; but I am persuaded that you are in some way the sweetest of sisters and girls, and a prisoner whom Serapis will not readily let go."

"But—let one look at you!"—and when Miss Eve exhibited herself, "Is this Eve?" the other asked, for Miss Eve was in a garb all of flimsies of the Orient as gaudy as rainbows—silk-muslins, gauzes—her ears gross with ear-rings of coral-rock and gold, a kefie-cloth draping her face, with her gazelle, her maids, her boy-poet wearing his embroidered sandals and strings of little pearls....

"Well, this is Eve," breathed Miss Ruth, musing upon the other with her bambino eyes, a smile of happiness chronic on her lips; "and whatever can that be on your nails?"

"Henna."

"Eve!"

Miss Eve snapped her thumb and finger gaily up in the air saying, "Oh, well, never say die, and in Rome let's row with the Romans; once I was queen of the Greeks, hundreds of eras ago. Come, sweet, to see the seraglio," and thither they hurried.

CHAPTER XV.

TO SHUNTER.

Lepsius, the Exhibition being now about to begin, should have been in Paris, but was at Serapis: and that was a true word of the gossip Nundcumar that woman works a relaxation in the screw of greatness, and taints its vein. Paris was strange; and the weather there "treacherous," as they say. Frequently each day Lepsius was in communication with Monsieur Fautras, his broker, and with Schuré, his chief engineer. A rumour was abroad that the last of the Moon Debenture Bills (asking the sanction of the Chamber to the issue of yet new stock to the tune of a milliard and a half) would hardly be carried, because of another rumour that the moon-structure itself was fated to failure: an event that must ruin very many investors. So the croakers and screamers arose and mouthed: the scheme, they screamed, was never sound; down all at once one day from par to 97 fell the stock; speeches breathing rage were everywhere being made, in the streets, on 'Change, in the Chamber; newspapers furious with froths of abuse—true Paris-babies, created to live three days—saw the light, cried, and died; pamphlets, pamphlets, flooded the cafés; Lepsius, men said, had fled.

In truth, Miss Ruth was at present no more a prisoner in Serapis, but roamed whithersoever she chose in and out of it, visiting the Breton peasants round about, the sick in Serapis, and corresponding whenever she chose with her parent, to whom she wrote that the angel of the Lord had broken the bars of her prison. On the whole, she was so well known, and with so much respect, to everyone in Serapis, that it may have been beyond the wit of Lepsius, had he willed it, to keep her strictly a prisoner. At any rate, the *émeute* thus suppressed did not recur; and Lepsius pondered this anon.

Little enough time had he for pondering, however. That forenoon of wet and wind the slump in moon-stock continued from 97 to 95, and at nine that night a crowd that had waited for hours outside the Palais-Bourbon in the storm, unharnessed the horses from Monsieur de Courcy's brougham, and brought the Minister home with hurrahs, because his thunder at the Debenture Bill had resulted in its overthrow.

"Well, at half after eight a messenger hastened to tell me that Isabeau Thiéry was about to mount the tribune, and to the Palais-Bourbon Pierre Huré and I set off in a fiacre, seeing on the way streams of people who were speeding to join the crowd that loitered round the House, without seeming to heed the showers and the noise of the wind. Having reasons of my own for not desiring to be seen within the Chambre des Députés itself, I strolled in the Salle des Pas Perdus, while Thiéry, ever the *enfant terrible* of the Députés, rolled his periods in the interior. Among us outside in the Pas Perdus the question was, 'Is Thiéry speaking for or in opposition to the Debenture Bill?' and managing to seize upon the old Major-General Dauriac, one of the three Quæstors, who came rushing in, I put to him the question. He shrugged both his shoulders on high, giving me the reply, 'Who knows, my friend? In the former half of his oration Thiéry has denounced the Bill, but now is no less loudly sounding its praises. *C'est un homme nul, ce monsieur-là*'—and he hastened on his way.

"I at once set out on the quest of Thiéry, wondering within myself how it was that Lepsius was not that night in Paris! Was it *because* of the very hardship of combating the storm from the place in which he happened to find himself that he decided to remain in it? Some stiffness of neck? Some arrogance? For he was arrogant. Nothing was greater than the grossness of his arrogance, save the glory of his lowliness. Seeing men, he felt himself a deity; but he was saved from even the least taint or vein of vanity, because his consciousness was so quick and large, that no less nearly and clearly than he saw men he saw stars, and felt himself a flea. At any rate, he could never be induced to take the human race quite *au sérieux*; he abided in his Brittany.

"When I flew to tell Lepsius of it, he during two seconds or so stood mute, then very hurriedly said, 'Thanks. I'll look to it'...."

What Lepsius did on learning of the disaster was urgently to telephone a certain course of conduct to an agent in Chantilly; he then at once summoned to his presence the Due de Rey-Drouilhet, who during two days had been staying at Serapis; and he took two pilules out of a cabinet and put them in a pill-box.

He turned to a servant by his elbow who bore him a leaf of ivory scribbled with these words: "Healy can live only a few minutes more.—RUTH."

Lepsius sprang up, pestered at this the third missive of the kind received that day, he having been too busy to pay any heed to them, though Healy was at this time, by his orders, near him in the north palace. He walked away to the columns, and cast a look out: no stars out there, no vault of heaven, only darksomeness mixed all with water and winds wawling; and back he bolted to the duke, saying, "Excuse me two minutes," and hastened away.

His own motive in going he hardly knew, since that was hardly very rational that he should go: but something that is in the breast brought him. However, he did not enter, only stole nigh, and, standing outside a doorhanging, listened, spied.

The two windows looked toward the coast, and though these were well closed, everything movable in the room moved to a breeze that ever breathed through it—the bed-curtains, the skirt of an Ursuline who kneeled near the bottom of the bed, telling her beads, the skirt of Miss Ruth who kneeled at the bed's head, reading, the beard of the old Nundcumar who sat leaning forward on a sofa between these two.

Miss Vickery held under her eyes on the bed's edge a Greek Bible from which with a poignancy and grieving in her voice she was translating, the gale battering anon great breaches in her speech in the ear of Lepsius.

"Nor be called masters ... but he that is greatest among you will be your servant ... and he that humbles himself is high."

The bed was low and small, in the north-west corner of the chamber under a window—the window which was opposite the door where Lepsius waited, there being two doors in the length of the room (which was longish and narrow), and two great windows, under a groined roof; and though an Arabian boy, crouching on a rug in the south-west corner of the marble floor, made a fourth watcher in the chamber, there was an air of loneness in there, an odour of death. This little Arab, indeed, but increased this feeling: for, though kneeling, he was so doubled on himself, so stone-still, that he seemed to be dead, and a greenish sheen gloating on his cheek from the lamp-globe just above his head increased his appearance of death.

"And they came to a place named Gethsemane, and he said to his disciples, 'You wait here, while I go to pray.'"

The light of the only lamp was somehow a local halo about itself, throwing the remainder of the room in some obscurity, so that the clicks of the nun's rosary arose from shadows in which she was herself no more than a shadow; nor could Healy be seen, nothing but his toes sticking up beneath the clothes, though anon that keen ear of Lepsius could hear his throat croaking the death-ruckle, pouring it low, hurried, like a purring rolling; and, still more pressed with haste, rain-water outside struggling darkly down spouts, with gulps and sobs and goblin sounds; and again that poignancy and break in Miss Vickery's voice....

"And he went a little onward, and dropped down upon the ground, and prayed, saying, 'Abba (papa), take away this cup from me; still, not what I want, papa, but what thou.'"

Loudly from across the sea came the sound of the gale, flapping with the sound of a navy of argosies going down in some archipelago of gloom, with all their great sails whooping loose, and all their sailors wailing.

"And again he went away, and dropped down on the ground, and prayed, saying, 'If it be possible, let this draught pass away from me; still, not what I want, papa, but what thou.'"

The hand of Lepsius tightened on the box that held the two pilules designed for Isabeau Thiéry's breakfast; at the same time the death-ruckle on the bed came on a sudden to an end; the happy saint raised herself from the bedside with a smile and a light in her eyes; and during some moments nobody moved in the room, until now the crony Nundcumar rose to move to the bed's head, and, bowed over the dead with a moving brow and body, crooning, he said, "He is dead. But his head is not yet thoroughly dead and done, and he lies reflecting dimly in himself, thinking: 'I am dead: no more to view the sight of the sun, nor any light of the moon at night, nor all the stars: for I am dead, and this is death; and what I long saw falling upon others, and was long in awe of for myself, is fallen at last this day upon me, me, also: for I lie dead, and this is my day.'"

As for Lepsius, he was gone; not so swiftly as he had come.

When he got back to the hall where the duke awaited him, he halted two seconds betwixt two of the columns, struck with hesitancy: until, suddenly running, he muttered, "Forgive me for being longer than I meant; and now, to catch the train, you should be in haste"—he held out the pill-box.

Lepsius' lip of disdain deigned no reply.

"I know it, of course," remarked the old fop piteously in a flurry, "and asked only for form's sake.... On those terms I am entirely at your service."

"Rey-Drouilhet, be certain and deft," said Lepsius impressively; and within eight minutes Rey-Drouilhet was on the way to the railway. Before 7.40 the following morning he sat, in the Rue de Rome, at Isabeau Thiéry's bed's head.

He pretended that pressing Serapis-gossip had thus brought him at the matin-gun; but he had hardly any need to invent the gossip, since by this time Thiéry could speak of nothing but Lepsius' bribe.

"My friend, what was the amount?" the duke questioned with a screwed countenance.

"It was two millions, monsieur."

"*De Dieu de Dieu!*... I who am no more a youth would undoubtedly have refused it without difficulty, but how could you, a young man?"

"Ah, mon cher ami, noblesse oblige," remarked Isabeau Thiéry in an absent mutter.

He was now about to get out of bed to get on his clothes, when his *gouvernante* bore him in his coffee and little loaf; and during the minutes that he took to fling on his things, the coffee stood cooling on a commode close to the duke. The flesh of the duke's face during this became very blanched and aged, his manners nervous and fluttered; but, though he had the two pills in his hand, and had many opportunities of dropping them into the coffee during Thiéry's dressing, he did not. He now thought to himself, "No, Thiéry must be out of the room," and presently he passed the remark that he had not breakfasted.

"My friend, pardon me!" cried out Thiéry, and darted out half-dressed to order another cup of coffee.

Now was the duke's opportunity. Yet he did not drop the pills into Thiéry's coffee. He started! First athwart the whirl of his thoughts flushed Isabeau Thiéry's words, "*noblesse oblige*," the example of that generous blood: and away he rushed, bent, from the coffee; and then back to it he rushed, fleet and thievish, to dash in the pills; and away from it afresh, without having dashed them in. And now he was casting his arms on high, his rickety eyes, distracted; and now he was creeping on his knees, sneakingly, to drop the two pills into a pot beneath the bed; and now he was at Thiéry's bread, sneakingly kneading two pills out of the pith; and *these* he dropped into Thiéry's coffee....

Later that forenoon he misquoted Shakespeare, despatching to Lepsius, in English, the telegram, "The deed is done."

Nor did Lepsius need the coming of this telegram to be perfectly certain that the deed was done, though he could scarcely still have been ignorant that very many threads congregate to make the mental texture of modern men. Anyway, till late in the day he was securely acting upon the fact that the duke could not fail; and then, suddenly, he knew—too late....

The next night, the second of the Exhibition, was the night on which men had been given to hope that a strange glory would change the look of the skies: but no such glory arose upon the eyes.

Lepsius smiled, but bitterly. He was lying on his belly on a bed of straw, reading the life of Jesus of Nazareth in the book of Matthew when the news of the destruction of the moon-offices reached him; and at once, throwing away the book to run out with a reddened brow, he said within himself, "I will blot out this name of France." During the rage and deluge of the few days following, he yet more hardened his heart. To Miss Ruth Vickery he refused an interview, and to Miss Eve Vickery, who wrote "I am sorry for you," and entreated him to be meek, to cease from scheming, and to bend his head before the tempest, he condescended to send no answer.

Never did Lepsius loom so hugely upon the universal world, luminous as some angel of the welkin, as that afternoon, France, for her part, casting upon her head the ashes of contrition. As for the foes of Lepsius, they saw only instant loss of place and power, only ruin, degradation, disgrace, knowing that now the decree of banishment against him was nothing but a dead letter. Hence the Count de Courcy took a hurried trip down into Brittany that day, and contrived to talk a little with the prattler Nundcumar outside the walls of Serapis....

At the moment when Lepsius went under the water for the second time, Nundcumar, suddenly grabbing the dog by the collar, coughed twice: and the next moment the dog broke roaring from his grasp to drag down a woman who rose out of the coffer and flew through the room....

Lepsius, hearing the row, reared up his head, and even as the woman went down under the hound, received vitriol about his brows....

He at once dived....

Later in the day he discovered that one of his sandals, in a chamber of which he kept a little key, was missing. It was the Abbé Sauriau who told him so, kneeling over Lepsius on his bed of straw, as the gloaming began to grow deep. "It is intended that your hoards shall be distributed among charitable institutions," the abbé said; and he cried accusingly, his body convulsed with sobs, "Lepsius, you are blind! and it is I who have been the cause of this."

Lepsius lay with a band covering his eyes, his limbs cast all asprawl at random, tossing for ease; and presently he bleated, "I am blind!"

And now Isabeau Thiéry, waiting for hours at the far end of the chamber, dashed both his palms to his ears to shut out the sound of that bleat, which each three minutes was repeated, and rushed with the stare of a maniac away.

Lepsius could get no rest, for though the ravage of the vitriol (thanks to the rush of the dog and to the bath-water) was local about the brows, and he was hardly at all disfigured in his face, yet the agony was great, and the heat of the atmosphere every moment growing greater, since a reign of licence and riot had kept carnival during all the afternoon, and at several places Serapis was flaring.

"You must not stay here much longer," blubbed the Abbé Sauriau, with two big tears streaming on his cheeks.... "I have a little cottage in Chantilly, and thither you will come to abide until my death by my side. You are poor, you are many millions in debt, you are utterly destitute, naught can be more utter, more boundless, than your downfall. So you will come, my friend, to my breast, and in the cottage we shall be, we two, dwelling in a shaded leisure and seclusion of literature, for I shall be reading my books to you, and you will be dictating books to me, which I shall write for you."

"I am blind!" bleated the blind boy to his obscurity, neither heeding nor hearing him.

"I shall never run again!" complained Lepsius to his gloom.

"You may! You do not know yet! God may will to give you back your eyes, or one of them! But say that you will come this night with me."

94

"Are you not still against me?" asked Lepsius in pain.

"What, against my own? Was I ever really against *you*, do you dream? Oh, fie, hard heart, to let yourself utter those words!"

Lepsius now turned a little to put his arm about the old man's shoulder, and water washed with a whey of blood wound all down one side of his nose, while the old man moaned.

"So, then," the old man said, "you will come, for I feel that it will do you good, and I'll go at once to see to it."

"Eve, I am blind!" bleated Lepsius aloud, perhaps having caught and known the sound of her walk, or probably invoking her without any knowledge that she was present; and what pen of poet or seer of the soul can disclose the olio of her whole emotion then, sketching with what fiendishness of hell-spite her whitened lip touched her lower teeth, as she flung at him, "You should have been good!" and then again how the bowels of her woman's ruth moved and rued, beholding him so low, when he rose on his elbow, but tumbled back, calling, "Eve! you are here!"

"Lepsius, I am going for good from you!"

"Eve, do not leave me!"

"Eve!" her father now called out in a sort of whisper.

Now, however, a crazy stare was gazing out of the carriage window, Miss Eve leaning out, saying, "Do you say, woman, that he forgave you? Oh, tell me the God's truth!"

"Why, yes, since you see me here——" the hag began to say: but now Miss Eve was gone.

"Eve!" howled her father after her, "remember your vow to——?"

Miss Eve threw her hand backward without looking round, and went fluttering on her way, her frocks quarrelling with the winds; nor was it possible to pursue her with the brougham, since she took a shortcut path through a meadow; and though her father and Miss Ruth ran after her, calling, her youth and long legs soon got them pretty far behind, she slipping back to Serapis like a spring which, pressed the wrong way, is of a sudden sprung free. In some fifteen minutes she lay on her love's bed, shuddering on his breast, her teeth chattering feverishly into his ear "for ever," and anew "for ever."

"Eve, you are here!" he called to her in that voice of the blind which has lost its way like a lambkin bleating in the void of the night; and she

95

in the fever of her joy said to him, "Here, you can feel it, the half coin: where should I be but in you, but interned in your heart, my eternal? I who eternities since yearned at the altar with you."

But now Dr. Lepsius walked actively in to announce that everything was ready as to the vessel; and about half an hour after this, a small crowd consisting of Dr. Lepsius, Lepsius, Miss Eve, Miss Ruth, Mr. Vickery, a Dr. Proudhomme of Serapis, the Abbé Sauriau, Isabeau Thiéry, Saïd Pasha, and Mr. E. Reader Meade, paced to the quay of the little bay named Petit Bazaine. Yonder on the sea the yacht's three lights glared tiny in a darkness made rather Tartarian by the conflagration of Serapis, the glows from which, glaring on the slopes of the billows' blackness in dabble-ments, gave to the bay the goriness of Aceldama. A boat lay at the end of the quay; but as the sea was very rough, and trouble was looked for in embarking Lepsius, all the party went forward to see the boat, leaving him seated alone on a block of stone. The boatmen, who lay on their oars, called that they would wait for a calmer moment; so it was some minutes ere Miss Eve ran back to bring Lepsius, and then to her amazement, met him on his knees—the roar of the breakers and of the gale in his ears, the sprays raining on his face, or his engrossment, may be, in his prayer, pre-venting him from hearing her approach. She with an uplifted hand, stood hushed a little, listening, catching some words, the bursting of his sobs.... "Who hearest, but dost not heed, the bleatings of brutes ... yet if just one human wish for once may move thee ... let no speck of grit ever prick her eyes to agonise her; oh, I was sick and she visited me pelt her; I am reft, despoiled, and she makes choice of me ... chase, infest her every hour with fresh showers and astonishments of joy——"

She touched him, saying, "Come."